Bait Wolf

Lunar City Fight League
Book 1

Sienna Sway

Contents

Chapter One

Coal

If you want your little sister back, you know what to do.

The words echoed in my mind like a record on repeat. Asha was more like a daughter to me than a little sister. She was twenty years younger, an accidental child from one of the whores in the red-light district.

Father should have known better, but I'd never actually blamed him for this particular mistake because the moment Asha was left on our doorstep, I had fallen utterly in love with her. I knew that she would be mine to care for, to love, and to keep safe, and I had done everything in my power to do just that.

Until now.

If you want your little sister back, you know what to do.

I lunged forward as those painful words continued to echo in my mind. I bypassed the gangsters that Harvey had gotten me involved with and went straight for the small man himself.

Harvey squeaked, throwing himself back but not fast enough. I caught him against the cold, damp wall and lifted him by the neck.

I was a monstrous being, in wolf and man form both; my stature, build, and ferocity had earned me the nickname the Redwood. I was thought to be huge and infallible. That was what they said about me whenever I entered the Lunar City Fight ring.

Although he was a wolf shifter too, my manager Harvey had always reminded me more of a rat. Always sniffing around for the next way to use me to make a few bucks. Normally I didn't give a fuck because it always paid out, but if my family was involved, that changed everything.

"What have you done?" I snarled.

Harvey whimpered and choked.

He couldn't answer because my grip was too tight. I was barely able to restrain myself. Oh, how easy it would be to snap that small frail neck.

For a moment, I saw red. My grip tightened. Harvey's face turned purple, his eyes bugging out.

A chuckle broke through the tension, and suddenly I remembered that we weren't alone.

I dropped Harvey like a rag, ignoring the coughing heap of a man, and turned to face the gangsters, the ones who had just told me they had taken Asha.

My fiery gaze landed on the two of them.

Brothers Alek and Kai Belkin were notorious in Lunar City, but they hadn't yet been caught or, at least, they had connections with the police that kept them free.

They were both big alphas. Not quite in my league, but there were two of them.

Alek, the older brother, shook his head.

"Calm down, okay? She's fine. Last I checked, she was eating pizza with her babysitter and watching *My Little Pony*."

The description of my little sister tugged at my

heart. She loved that annoying show. I would literally give my right arm to be sitting with her, watching it, my big arm around her small shoulders. To get her back, I would do anything they asked.

I felt my shoulders sag at the realization, and a look of glee passed over the brothers' faces.

"What do you want from me?" I growled.

The edge of threat in my voice was useless; they already knew they had won.

"You know what we want," Kai said. "Lose the fight. Simple as that."

"How do I know I'll get her back?"

"She'll be there."

"At the fight?" I asked, heart racing. "To see me *lose?*"

The brothers shrugged.

"And as soon as you do, you can take her home," Alek said. "But *only* if it looks believable."

"We wouldn't do anything in front of such a big crowd, would we?"

I looked at each of them in turn, even turning to give Harvey a disgusted glare. He was still a simpering lump on the floor, his cheap suit dirtied by the mold on the wall.

I didn't trust any of them, not one bit, but I didn't have a choice, did I?

I'd never lost a fight in my career yet. When the gates opened and I faced my opponents, something came over me. The true wild nature of my wolf completely took control. Then again, that was the whole point, wasn't it? When wolves lost it, the bloody display was all the entertainment one could ask for.

"So, do we have a deal?"

Alek came forward, offering his hand.

For a minute, I didn't move. I didn't know if I could control myself when it came down to it. Then again, I *had* to.

I didn't want Asha to see me getting torn apart whether it was agreed upon or not, but there was no other way.

I reached forward and took the offered hand in an iron grip.

"Bring her to the fight."

"She'll be there." Alek grinned.

Dropping the slimy grip from my own, barely able to contain the rage of twisting emotions, I shouldered past them to the door, pausing to turn and look back at them.

"Pull any strokes and I'll annihilate Lambert and come after each of you personally."

Harvey and Kai paled and, if I wasn't mistaken, a

twitch of apprehension ran over even Alek's face.

I slammed the thick metal door behind me and took off, marching through the dank corridors.

The fight league had become my savior in many ways, taking me beyond the limits of the life I'd known. By now, I was familiar with every part of this dirty business. Normally I chose to look at the good and turn my cheek to the bad. Well, that was hard to do right now.

I was currently in the Lunar City Fight League's underbelly, a system of damp cement corridors and rooms that hid all sorts of unpleasantness from the rest of society. Above was the stadium, an enclosed fight ring with thousands of seats rising on all sides.

The semi-legal fights were a national sensation that drew crowds unlike any other sport. And off the blood of pack shifters, a lucky few made a killing. It was a true display of the depravity of wolves, and down here, where the true dregs of society ran business, I was normally one of the star players. After all, I was the current favorite. Thirty professional wins, zero losses.

That was why they wanted me to lose. Throw the fight so they could make millions on their bet... How much was Harvey getting out of this arrangement, I wondered.

Somewhere in the distance, a shout of fear echoed through the passages from some unknown location. How many people were being wronged, tortured, maybe even murdered down here?

A flash of familiar guilt hit me then, but as always, I pushed the feeling down, allowing anger to overtake it.

I needed a way to provide for my sister. Without an education or status, this was what I'd come up with: using my strengths, and I was a fighter through and through.

Normally, omegas were the key. They were brought in to use as bait wolves, to stoke the flames of competition between the fighters, but I didn't need them. In the moment, when another alpha ran for the omega, yeah, it felt wrong, like I should be the one winning them, but even without an omega's presence, I could still rip the head off any wolf out there.

After the fights, I'd known winners and losers both who sometimes obsessed over the omega they'd nearly had. Sometimes they were even sold to fighters for the right price. Often, they were too badly mangled during the event to even survive.

The fact that people were being trafficked for this sport didn't seem to bother anyone, but I couldn't help glancing down the halls now, wondering where all the stolen omegas were being kept.

A life in a cell was not one worth living anyway. Maybe death was a relief.

Maybe Asha is down here.

The thought made my step falter, nearly sending me back down the stairs just as I started to ascend them, ready to go on a rampage looking for her.

No. If she was in the maze of tunnels down here, I would never find her. Best to wait until tomorrow, to have this fight with Lambert. If she was in the middle of the crowd, nothing could be done to her.

Gritting my teeth, I went up the stairs, all the way to the back exit, and emerged into the evening light.

Lunar City was full of back alleys like these. Dark and dank, the opposite of what the beautiful skyline and shining lights would have you believe.

Once upon a time I'd been part of the bottom drudges. To rise to the top, I'd nearly gotten myself killed in the ring and nearly killed my opponents as well.

I'd done it all for Asha. I rubbed shoulders with the upper crust of society, the Lunar City aristocrats, and I'd bought us a big house on the outskirts with a big yard for her to play in.

Now I wondered if any of it was worth it.

I would survive the day without Asha, lose that fight, and then everything would go back to normal.

Chapter Two

Ember

My body rattled from the cold. I was so thin now that I didn't doubt that the clinking of bones was audible through the thin layers of my skin.

No muscle or fat remained to warm me or offer any comfort from the icy cement of the cell I had called home for too long.

The cold was worse than the pain. In the end, it was harder to adjust to. The sharp sting of broken bones, scrapes, cuts, and deep gouges—all of it was so familiar it was almost a comfort to me now. If I remained still, the sharpness of fresh pain dulled and slowly faded.

Being a shifter meant I healed faster than a regular human or wolf did, but I couldn't help but notice that, over the months that had passed, my healing had slowed down as my body had become ever frailer and weaker.

At first, I'd fought tooth and claw for freedom. Then I'd accepted this fate... Now, I knew that had been a mistake.

There would never be an end to this suffering, except with my death.

I had thought that if I gave in, I would be treated better. That hadn't happened. Instead, I'd lay down and allowed my life to dwindle to its near end.

Any day now, I would be brought into another fight. I wouldn't survive the next one; of that, I was sure.

I twisted on the hard, damp floor, naked in my human form, too weak to shift into my wolf for the small bit of relief that my fur would offer. My gaze landed on the grate above.

It led onto a street, maybe a back alley. I wasn't sure, except that trucks often passed overhead, blocking out the light of day and the streetlights at night. On occasion, I heard people talking, but if they heard my shouts for the first endless months I'd been here, they didn't care to respond.

Not surprising, really. Lunar City was like that. It was a big, bustling city, packed with the supernatural. Wolf shifters ran the place. Growing up on the streets had taught me a long time ago that I'd rather take my chances with actual wild animals than the scum that lived here.

I'd been so confident back then. Thought I knew the ways of the streets like the backs of my hands. I'd seen kids go missing on more than one occasion. I assumed the worst. Still, I never once thought that *I* would be taken. Even though I knew about the fight league, I'd never even considered that I would end up being a bait wolf for it.

A rattle of chains drew me from my thoughts. I looked over at the door as it opened, revealing a sight that drew my interest enough that I attempted to sit up. It took two tries and a hiss of pain, but I was upright by the time my visitors entered. One was my usual guard, a frail man who never made eye contact when he brought small bits of food or water to my cell. I couldn't help thinking he felt guilty. That didn't mean he was going to quit though. He probably did this as a job to make ends meet, surely earning a pathetic excuse of a wage.

The other two large alphas who entered were far more interesting. Abram Adair himself, creator of the Lunar City Fight League. He was the showrunner, the man on the absolute top. He looked it too, with silky blond hair, large white teeth, and cruel eyes. What was he doing here?

The man he led in after him, I didn't recognize, but that didn't mean I couldn't read power when I saw it, and it had nothing to do with the perfect cut of his expensive suit or the way he sneered down at me. It was in the very way he carried himself.

"This is the last one," Abram said to the man. His assessing gaze never moved from me where I crouched in the corner in rags. Finally, he shook his head, pulling a handkerchief from his pocket and covering his nose at my stench. "It won't do. He's not good enough. I'll find you a fresh omega, one worth fighting over."

Anger I didn't know I was even capable of feeling again lanced through me, so sharply that I began to shake.

"Wait."

The other man bent down, still far enough back that I couldn't quickly reach him—as though I had the strength to attack anyone right now.

His gaze seemed to peer straight through me. Finally, he straightened, nodding thoughtfully.

"This is the one."

"Alek, you can't be serious. Look at him."

"This is the one," he insisted. "He's weak, but there's fight in him. Lambert likes a fiery damsel. This one wants to survive. Don't you, little pup?"

"I'm not a pup!" I snapped, my voice a sharp whip that scratched over my throat, leaving it immediately hoarse and in pain.

Alek laughed. The sound was loud and jarring after so long in the near silence of my cell.

He turned to Abram smugly.

"Have him cleaned up for the fight and he'll be perfect. He'll definitely have them drawing blood."

Abram nodded, sparing me only one last dubious glance as they left my cell.

The guard locked the door firmly after their departure, the familiar sound of the chains being fastened from the corridor chilling me even more than the icy cement.

This was it. They'd written my execution.

I was fiery by nature, that was true, but after being here for so long, I had thought the last flames within me had already been put out. I was surprised that man, *Alek*, had seen it so readily in me. It sickened me to think that my desire to live would be the thing to inevitably end me.

I couldn't survive another fight. I knew that much. An alpha overcome by an omega's presence in the middle of a heated situation like a fight... Well, they couldn't often control themselves. Often the omega ended up shredded up in the process of two alphas trying to win them.

I knew from experience. From the terrifying moments I'd been cornered like a wild animal just before they lost all sense of themselves, I would do anything to escape facing it again.

This was my last chance. By tomorrow evening, I would escape, or I would die.

Chapter Three

Ember

I fell into a fitful sleep sometime later, telling myself that I needed to sleep to collect my strength. If I didn't, I wouldn't be able to walk away, let alone run.

When I thought about running, panic filled me. I wanted freedom more than I wanted anything, even life. If I was going to die, I wanted it to be on my own terms, *fighting*, not at the hands of an organization and a city that had failed me.

How could I escape though? When would I be left unattended? Every other time, I had been escorted to the event in chains that weren't removed until I was *in* the fight ring. What made me think this time would be any different?

The answer came when I was awakened by the familiar sound of rattling chains and my door being yanked open.

My heart jumped with fear, pounding so hard that I thought I might choke on it.

I didn't have a plan yet. It couldn't be time already!

The guard held the door open for me.

"Come on," the frail man muttered.

It took several tries for me to get to my feet. My body creaked and ached. When I fell for the second time, another man entered with an impatient huff.

He took me roughly by the arms, clearly more concerned with his time than the state of his charge, and hoisted me through the door.

Down the hall I was dragged, feet barely managing to find purchase on the damp floor until eventually, I realized that they were not taking me in the usual direction. I wasn't being taken to the stadium for the fight.

Instead of asking, I bit my lip, eyes wide, as I was taken this way and that through the corridors and then up a long narrow staircase.

At the top, in a much cleaner, drier corridor, our

journey continued. The floors here were carpeted and the air warm. The feeling of my toes scraping over the soft surface was almost pleasurable. Doors that I peeked through with wide eyes offered glimpses of sunlight through the windows.

My breath caught at the beauty of the orange glow of natural light. So beautiful.

I had always taken for granted the lovely warmth of the sun. If I got out of here alive, I would relish it. I could see it now, a spot in the woods, away from these people where I could sit in patches of sun that shone through the leaves of the trees. I could have a cabin maybe, hidden where no one could ever reach me. Especially alphas.

Finally, my escort stopped, opened a nondescript door, and pushed me through it.

I stumbled on my weak feet and didn't even have the chance to catch myself before the door shut behind me.

Two thin arms suddenly came around me, catching me and steadying me. This time, they were gentler than the last set that had dragged me.

When I looked up, I was surprised to meet kind eyes, pale blue—nearly white—that were fixed on me with something like pity and fear intertwined.

Another omega.

Not a bait wolf though, that was clear, although, at first glance, I would bet he was being kept against his will. For one, his room didn't appear to have a window. He was slender, but not malnourished the way that I knew I was myself, and he wasn't riddled with scars and wounds either.

"Are you okay?" the other omega asked gently, then tutted before I could answer. "No, of course you're not. I shouldn't have asked."

Helping me walk, he led me through the bedroom, through a side door that opened into a bathroom where a bubble bath was already waiting.

A hoarse laugh left my mouth, scratching my throat even worse than before.

"Is this for me?" I asked.

"I'm going to help you get cleaned up," the other omega said, "for the event."

"My death, you mean."

My voice was barely a whisper now, so unused to being used, but with his sharp wolf hearing, the other omega had no issue catching it.

"Not necessarily," he said, averting his gaze.

Clearly choosing not to continue the conversation, he began to help me undress. What had once been clothes, perhaps slacks and a t-shirt—I couldn't remember—were now nothing but scraps of fabric

20

that had been tied in places to stay on. When one knot couldn't be undone, the other omega extended a claw, easily slicing through the fabric and letting it fall around my bony ankles.

I couldn't complain. Truthfully, I was eyeing the bath almost lustfully. I couldn't remember the last time I had felt warm.

Carefully, the omega helped me step into the fragrant bubbles. I nearly melted in appreciation as I sank tired bones into the water and felt the warmth envelop me and the pressure ease off my joints.

For a moment, this simple, *normal* experience— another thing that I had taken for granted in the past —was so overwhelming that tears sprang to my eyes. I bowed my head, sobs suddenly raking my tired form as I lamented all that I had lost, all that had been taken from me.

When I finally managed to lift my head again, the other omega was gone. I was alone in the wash-room, although the door had been left open and I could hear clattering in the other room. In front of me, to my shock, was a frosted window that I hadn't taken notice of before. It was high up and small, but I was quite small now too. I could easily fit through it. *If* I knocked out my current companion and then hoisted myself up there, of course. The idea was laughable. I could barely even stand.

"Here."

The omega's return drew my attention from the flimsy plan to a mouthwatering sight. He had a full platter of food for me. More than I had seen in so long and it all looked so fresh, so delicious. Strawberries, apples, and grapes.

The platter was placed on the edge of the tub. I didn't know what to reach for first. My hand landed on a strawberry. The moment it touched my tongue, I thought I might start crying again.

"What's your name?"

I glanced at the omega who was watching me with such soulful, sad eyes that for a moment I felt bad for him being in this situation. It wouldn't be easy to prepare others of your kind to be placed in such danger.

I swallowed the grape currently in my mouth, an explosion of flavor.

"Ember."

My voice was already a tiny bit stronger. A small smile touched the other omega's lips.

"That suits you," he said. "It matches your eyes."

My eyes. I used to get so many comments about them, that they were the color of embers, dark and orange with a golden glow. I'd even been told, a long time ago, that they blazed when I got angry.

I swallowed back the old memory, my mother's voice echoing in my ears.

"What's your name?" I asked, remembering the order of conversing a little too slowly. The omega didn't seem to mind though.

"Maple," he said softly. Then, seeing that the fruits were nearly all gone, "I'll get you something more substantial when you're ready. What would you like?"

"I can have anything?" I asked uneasily.

"Of course."

"Like a last meal?"

His face paled.

"No, that's not what I meant..."

We both fell silent and after a moment of stillness, he went behind me and grabbed the shampoo bottle.

"You don't mind, do you?" he asked.

I shook my head.

I was sure Maple had been given orders. They wanted me cleaned up, after all. Still, I appreciated that I was being asked as though I had a choice.

Truthfully, it had been so long since anyone had touched me with gentleness and kindness that it felt nice. A shiver traveled through me as my hair was washed and rinsed. Maple took great care with it, being as gentle as he could. When he was done, he asked me if he could cut it. Again, I knew it wasn't up to me, but I nodded and relaxed back, my eyes drooping in a moment of peace I hadn't felt in too long.

When he was done with the razor and scissors, he tried to wash my body, but I drew the line there. It was nice to be cared for, but I could do it myself.

I took my time with the cloth and soap, noting the way the water was beginning to turn gray as layers of filth came off me.

It was strange, surreal really, and so very easy to shut my eyes and forget about everything but the relief in my body and my mind—no matter how short lived it would be.

When I was helped to stand, a soft towel was offered to me. When I was dried, I was given clothes that were even softer.

Maple gave me some privacy while I changed. Again, I could hear the soft clattering of dishes from the other room and my stomach rumbled from the thought of more food, despite how digesting the fruit I had eaten was already proving a struggle after so long with so little.

Leaning against the cold marble of the sink, I pulled the cotton pants up my thin legs. The shirt was a bit easier to do up. When my gaze landed on a pair of fluffy white slippers, a smile touched my lips.

I slipped my feet in, reveling in the warmth after a minute of standing on the cool tiles.

How would I ever go back to that cold cell after this?

The smile dropped from my face.

I wasn't meant to, was I? That was the whole point of this. This was really meant to be my last little bit of time on earth.

My gaze flew to the window. I *could* fit.

Edging toward the door, I couldn't even see where Maple was. He was in a different room somewhere, preparing my last meal.

Fuck that!

Adrenaline shot through my body.

With a sudden hunger for life I didn't know I still possessed, I stumbled to the window.

I was clean and dressed. Even my aches were diminished from the warmth of the water I'd soaked in.

This moment was my best—my *only*—chance.

I hoisted myself onto the counter, weak arms shaking, and stood. I yanked the window, then had to jiggle it, rattling the glass in an effort to get it open. Suddenly, it slid up with full force, banging against the frame and I slipped. The soap dispenser fell to the floor, clattering loudly against the tiles.

Maple's worried voice came at once, drawing nearer.

"Ember?"

Shit.

I grabbed the edge of the window frame, scrambling, pushing, kicking, doing everything he could to hoist myself up there. *Finally*, my ribs went through the narrow gap and then my waist.

I was outside! Half of me, anyway. The window led into an alley crowded with garbage bins and parked cars. The drop below would be hard asphalt, but this was the ground floor, and it wasn't that far down.

A loud gasp behind me alerted me to Maple's arrival. Too late. All I had to do was fall.

I threw myself with all the strength I had left.

For a few seconds, I was free. The wind whipping through the alley hit my body and combed through my damp hair. The smells of garbage and car exhaust and other familiar, unpleasant but welcome, things enveloped me. Then, something wrapped around my calves, and I lurched to a stop.

Maple gripped my legs with such strength that, for a moment, I could do nothing but hang half out the window and shout.

"No! Let me go! Please!"

I struggled. Oh, I fought! With every ounce of strength that I had in my poor, pathetic body, I fought.

It didn't matter. Even as I was pulled back into the bathroom, even as I clung to the rotting frame, crying and begging, it made no difference.

"Please, just let me go," I sobbed.

I fell into the washroom. Maple went down with me and us two omegas, both slaves, cried on the bathroom floor.

"I'm sorry," Maple kept saying. "I'm so sorry."

A loud bang and thundering footsteps drew our attention, and only then did Maple pull himself together enough to stand, just as one of the guards came barreling into the doorway.

He stopped dead, taking in the scene, gaze flying to the open window and the two of us with red eyes and wet cheeks.

"Everything's okay," Maple said. "I have it under control. You can go."

The guard hesitated, then seemed to pull himself together.

"Get ready. I saw his escorts coming down the hall before I heard the commotion and ran in here. They'll be here any second to take him."

Maple nodded resolutely and waited for the guard to leave before turning back to face me.

"Come on," he said softly and dragged me to my feet.

He steered me to the front door.

I thought about fighting. One solid punch to the face might knock Maple out. I had almost been free. All I needed was a minute—but the doors flew open and my escorts, two solid-looking betas, walked in.

My steps faltered.

Maple didn't seem to want to push me forward. His hands shook on my back.

"I really am sorry," he whispered. "It's either you or me."

With that small admission, the desire to fight Maple seeped out of me.

I stepped forward.

My escorts each took one of my arms and steered me away from him and his guard.

Back through the corridors, back down that dark staircase to a more familiar landscape; the Lunar City Fight League's underbelly. The system of

28

tunnels and corridors and cells that had become my home.

Maple was living in luxury by comparison; he was healthy, fed regularly, had a kitchen and bathroom and even a bed. He wouldn't be able to handle the things that I had already endured or would endure.

I was already weak. I was on the verge of death. If one of us had to do this, better me than Maple.

But if this was my legacy, my ending, then one thing was for sure: no matter how big or how strong the alphas I would face were, I would not go down without a fight.

Chapter Four

Coal

I paced the back room like a caged animal. It was exactly what I would be soon enough, when they released me into that fight ring, and it was already exactly how I felt.

In the stadium beyond, I could hear thousands of people. Their seats rose above me, but as much as I wanted to see Asha, I couldn't go out there yet.

I wasn't alone. My team was all with me. The other alphas that I usually trained with were normally there to pump me up and help me get ready, but this time none of them approached me.

They could all tell I wasn't myself today. I hadn't slept a wink last night. I hadn't been able to. I'd been too angry. Normally rest and recovery was important leading up to a fight, but this time, it didn't matter. Not when I was planning to lose it anyway.

I still couldn't quite believe that my own manager had sold me out in exchange for a cut of this twisted deal. Whenever I thought of it, my claws kept extending spontaneously, fury pumping through me. I could barely contain my wolf at all.

I was so angry I didn't know how the hell I was going to walk into that ring and not completely lose it on Lambert.

If not for the fact that they had Asha, I would tear the other alpha limb from limb simply because I was in that mood.

A strong hand landed on my shoulder, and I swung without thinking. Luckily, my friend Everest was as quick as he was large, and the big man managed to duck out of the way.

"Careful there," he said, holding up his hands, baring his wrists and showing that his claws were withdrawn.

"You should know better than to sneak up on me," I growled anyway. "Especially right now."

"He didn't," Seymour said from the other side of the room.

Seymour and Everest always backed each other, so I only glared over at him at his interference.

"I said your name several times," Everest insisted. "So did *he*."

I looked where Everest gestured, toward the door, surprised by the presence of one of the club employees.

"Five minutes until your fight," the beta said awkwardly.

I managed to nod before looking around at my other friends.

Seymour, Aspen, and Aurora shrugged helplessly.

"We'll make sure they don't leave with Asha," Seymour said. "I'm watching the front door, and Aurora will be on the back door."

She nodded in agreement.

"And I'll be in your corner, as usual," Everest added.

They had offered to do more when I'd updated them, such as going as a team to tear down every door in the city until they found her.

I loved the sentiment, but if I could somehow get

Asha back while protecting her from seeing anything too violent, then that was the way to do it.

Seeing me get cut up wasn't exactly much better, but at least it was in a controlled environment.

Five minutes until we would see each other...

Every single one of those minutes seemed to drag on forever.

Finally, the crowd began to cheer, and music played. Lambert was emerging.

I was so eager, I felt like my skin was on too tight, like I was ready to burst free and tear through the aisles to that familiar cage—but only after I saw Asha. Once I'd seen her and that she was okay, then I would commit to this charade.

The door swung open again, and the club employee nodded for me to go.

I heard my music come on. The song was an old classic, a piano piece that rose in a crescendo as I walked through the hall and into the stadium. Because I was dramatic like that and this part, just like the fight itself, was about entertaining the crowd.

The lights were low, flashes of blue and pink neon as I walked into the open, and the whispered anticipation of the crowd erupted into a full-blown cheer. They were so loud that the sound reverberated through me, straight into my bones, filling me with an energy unlike anything else. The heady scent of so many wolves, so many mixed pheromones was dizzying. A delightful high when you were in the right mindset. Sometimes when I walked out into the crowd, between the aisles with the lights and cameras on me, I felt like I could do anything.

I shut my eyes, for a moment forgetting that this wasn't going to be like my other fights.

This one would end my winning streak but hopefully not my career.

When I opened my eyes again, my gaze settled on the cage in front of me. The familiar fight ring was lined to the ceiling with metal mesh. In a fight once, my opponent had climbed halfway up it in his attempts to get away from me.

Silvain "the Savage" Lambert was already in his corner, standing behind the waiting gate, stretching from side to side, nervous energy buzzing through his body. He looked on edge, even from here. Didn't he know that he was going to win? He must have. I'd bet that the bastard got a cut of the winnings.

I shut the thought down quickly. I was already angry enough. If I lost control now, there would be no way for me to throw the fight. I had to do this for Asha.

But as I reached the cage, fear struck me. I wasn't getting in until I saw her.

I spun around, unsure who to reach out to, struck by a helplessness I hadn't felt since childhood. But just as I turned my back to the ring, she was presented to me.

Out of nowhere, it seemed, two men parted, and Asha was there, between them. She was holding her lamb teddy and smiling up at me with her large, round eyes.

"Coal!" she squealed and leaped into my arms as I bent down, overcome by relief.

"Baby girl!"

My whole body was shaking as I held her and inhaled her sweet, innocent scent. All the tension inside me turned into mush as her small arms came around my neck, squeezing tightly.

"Are you okay? Did they do anything to you?"

She didn't seem to catch my meaning.

"We went to the science museum, and I played with the giant bubbles!"

"All right, that's enough. Let your daddy get to his fight and you can talk after."

One of the men tugged her back and only the fact that there were thousands of people watching stopped me from snapping on the spot. Not to mention the fact that I was *never* violent in front of Asha.

I stood up, looking down at the two men who had her, only now registering that they were Kai and Alek themselves. Of course. They wouldn't want me to know who her handler was, would they? Just in case I retaliated.

Neither of them said anything, just nodded to me. I watched sharply as they retreated to their seats, keeping Asha between them.

It did mollify me the slightest bit that I could see them. Their seats were only a couple rows back. Even if Asha was frightened seeing this fight, especially seeing me lose, I would make it up to her somehow.

"Ready?" Everest asked, drawing my attention back to the matter at hand. I nodded and climbed into my corner as the announcer shouted my name.

"Coal *the Redwood* Kent!"

The crowd was deafening, cheering for me, expecting another bulldozing win. I would put on a show. I had decided that yesterday, but when Lambert offered me something, a strong hit, a vicious bite, I would let the other wolf take me down. If I had to stare into little Asha's eyes the whole while, I would, just to remind my wolf why I could not keep fighting.

Taking a deep, steadying breath, I faced forward, gaze fixed on my opponent through my gate. They were made of metal, one on each side, thick enough to hold us in until the fight started, but with large enough gaps that we could smell the omega when they were brought in.

I had always found this to be an unnecessary part of the tradition. Bringing out the omega to convince the alphas to fight—as though they needed a reason.

As always, I fixed my gaze on my opponent, a stillness settling over me.

Lambert really was nervous. I could see it from here. The fear in his eyes when his unsteady gaze flickered in my direction filled me with confidence and eagerness. He knew he was going to win but he still didn't trust me, and I was going to use that. I was going to hurt him first, just for being a part of this.

The omega's entrance opened.

Hurry up, I thought. *Get this stupid ritual over with and let us fight!*

There was a moment's pause and then, finally, the omega entered.

And everything changed.

He was a slight creature, probably tall, but hunched and limping, a mass of swarthy skin and jagged, bulging bones. He tripped into the ring as though he was pushed into it, which was probably exactly the case, and he swung around, facing Lambert first. Then, just as swiftly, turned to face me.

He looked me straight in the eye. His glittering, fiery orange, which seemed to actually flicker in the light, met my somber gray.

The omega was like a mouse placed in a cat's trap, weak and delicate, and yet he tilted his chin up, a defiant look in those striking eyes like he wasn't completely out of his league.

Dumbstruck, I stared, unable to look away as my whole world tilted. The omega continued to turn, trying to keep each of us in his sight while the crowd roared.

There were three things that I knew at that moment. First, the omega was planning to fight back. If either of us got too close to him, or if he ended up in the crossfire of our fight, he would give back as much as he could. Second, he was prepared to die right here and now. And third, I would give my own life to save him because we were fated mates.

I'd heard stories that sounded like they were fairy

tales, of fated mates finding each other and knowing at first glance that their souls were connected and their love eternal. All my life, I'd never understood how they really *knew*. Now I did.

Suddenly a loud bell signified the start of the fight. The gates swung open.

Lambert emerged into the ring, intent on the omega, who backed away, eying us both with full-blown fear in his eyes.

I couldn't let the other alpha near my omega.

That was the last conscious thought I had.

Chapter Five

Ember

The alphas burst into the ring. I fell back, stumbling against the ropes, sure that they were going to jump me as one.

The one they'd called the Savage *did* run straight for me.

The weak ones always did. But the other one, the Redwood, beat him.

Already against the ropes, I ducked down. I couldn't shift in my state, but my claws managed to slice through my fingertips, ready to swipe—except that the Redwood's back was to me.

Shocked, I stared at him, unsure for a moment of what was happening. Then I realized: The Redwood was standing like a shield between me and the other alpha.

Usually, when an alpha wanted to show his dominance, that meant winning the omega, claiming them with bites and scenting, although they didn't often get to that stage during a fight. In this moment, it almost looked like the Redwood was *protecting* me.

It didn't make any sense, but each way the Savage moved, the Redwood met him.

Still in their human forms, they paced, the Redwood matching each move the Savage made. Their gazes were locked, reading each other intently.

The tension in the air was thick, and the crowd felt it. I could hear the commentators' urgent voices. Something about how they'd never seen the Redwood like this. Beyond them, the crowd reacted audibly to every sudden movement.

I stayed low, crouched small but alert, adrenaline pumping through my body. I didn't know what was happening exactly, except that soon, one of them would snap and I would be stuck in here with them.

Sure enough, with a frustrated growl, the Savage transformed. Fur sprang from his skin, his body distorting into a large, ferocious wolf. As soon as he did, the Redwood followed his lead, shifting into his wolf, dusky gray, huge, and even angrier.

It was hard to tell who jumped first, the Savage or the Redwood, but both lunged forward.

The crowd erupted into a cheer as the two alphas fell into the middle of the ring, jaws snapping as they rolled together.

My heart soared with hope.

Was that it? Was I free to go?

Normally once the fight got going, depending on the state of the omega, they were ushered from the ring. After all, they were only there to get the fight started, to give the alphas something they'd be willing to draw blood over.

I edged toward the omega door, eyes still glued to the fight.

One of the stadium workers snapped the lock up and motioned for me to hurry, and I nearly tripped over myself in my eagerness to get out.

I'd thought this was it for me.

Everything had suggested this would be my ending, and yet somehow, I was walking out unscathed.

The alphas didn't want me.

Relief unlike anything I'd ever felt was already overwhelming me as I turned to the door.

The sudden shout of the crowd was what alerted me that something was wrong.

In the split second that I reached the door, just as my foot passed through the threshold, the beta holding the door looked over my shoulder in horror and slammed the door shut, just as teeth scraped my arm through the thin fabric of my shirt and I was yanked away from it.

My whole body was thrown back through the air before landing with a heavy thud.

For a moment, I stared up at the lights, winded, spots exploding around me from the impact. Then I realized what had happened; I was in the center of the ring. One of the alphas—the Redwood—was standing over me on all fours, blood dripping from the ends of his gray fur. His entire face was red from it.

When I turned my head, I saw the other one— the Savage—cowering in a corner.

The fight was over. It had to be. The Redwood had won, but he wasn't trying to claim me and he wasn't backing down either. He stepped over me, legs on each side of my body and continued to growl, a deep, low, resonating sound that cut through all the other noise. He stared at the Savage as though his very presence was too close to me. A threat that had to be taken care of...

And although the Savage cowered, deferring to the Redwood with his nose nearly on the floor, blood soaking the ring around him, a loud whine leaving his throat, it didn't seem to matter.

The Redwood pounced.

People were screaming and shouting, some in horror, but mostly in excitement as the Redwood tore into the other alpha's flesh.

Disgust and terror overwhelmed me. For a moment, I couldn't move, watching in horror, and then, I couldn't *stop* moving, crawling away on shaking hands and knees toward the door again.

"He doesn't seem to be in his right mind—" The excited voices of the commentators cut through the uproar. "He's taken a liking to the omega—"

With a roar, the Redwood lunged at me.

I fell back with a shout. A tickle ran over my skin, my body attempting to shift, a last-ditch effort to protect me, but I couldn't do it and collapsed onto the mat as the Redwood reached me and—

Didn't touch me. Instead of attacking me, as I'd been so sure he would, the Redwood swung around, simply blocking my escape.

My entire body was abuzz with adrenaline and fear... and confusion.

I met the alpha's gaze.

Even in wolf form, even out of his mind, the alpha's eyes did something to me. They were familiar, like an old song, and a painful longing for something unknown enveloped me.

For a moment, I forgot everything. And then the shit hit the fan.

The fight was over, the other alpha was on the floor, unconscious and bloody. If he was still alive, it was hard to tell. Still, the Redwood wouldn't let anyone into the cage. The moment the doors opened, he snarled; if they dared set foot inside, he attacked before rushing back to me as though someone else might get me.

I remained very, very still.

From the sides, people coached me and told me not to move or antagonize the Redwood, or *Coal*, as some were calling him. His teammates and the club officials and eventually the club owner, Abram himself, got involved. All the while, the crowd watched with bated breath for what would happen next.

Eventually, someone arrived with a gun.

My heart stopped when I saw it.

"What are you doing?" I demanded.

My voice was shaking, and the Redwood crowded closer to me, his soft fur brushing my bare arms.

"Don't worry, it's a tranquilizer," someone told me from the outside of the ring.

I looked at the man who was trying to keep me calm. He was an alpha, large and broad. He looked like a fighter and, judging by the fact that he was in Coal's corner, he probably was. *Why* he thought that I would be worried about the Redwood, I was unsure, except that, for a moment there, I *had* been.

Without replying, I turned and watched as the gun was aimed straight at us. From this angle, so close to the large wolf's side, it looked almost like I was the one who would be shot.

When the man pulled the trigger, I jerked and the Redwood flinched, his entire body going rigid.

For a moment, he snarled, spinning to face the direction he had been shot from, ready to snap at whoever was there. With no one to attack, he turned around in a full circle, his sharp gaze going foggy, his movements slow.

With a low growl from deep in his belly, he crowded me all the way back against the corner and laid his huge form down in front of me.

He continued to growl even as his eyes began to droop.

Finally, I thought I might be free. When the gates opened and people entered, they went to the other alpha first, lifting the Savage's body onto a stretcher and quickly carrying him out.

I stayed where I was, partially because the Redwood had leaned his weight onto my legs, but also because I didn't know what to do.

Another stretcher was brought in, for the Redwood this time. He appeared to be asleep, but the moment he was touched by the two medics, his head lifted with another snarl.

"Don't worry," the one by his face reassured him, "We're bringing the omega with you."

Almost immediately, the alpha's head fell down heavily.

"You don't mean that, do you?" I asked as they lifted him onto the stretcher.

The Redwood opened his eyes and fixed his hazy gaze on me. He seemed to say, without words, *you're not leaving my side.*

Until I was told to come along, every time they moved, the prone alpha found the strength to growl at the men pushing him away.

Finally, when I grabbed onto the edge of the gurney, he seemed to relax.

"Congratulations, it looks like you found yourself an alpha."

I looked up at the voice. Abram smiled at me tersely. The club owner, the very man responsible for the fights and the deaths, the man who profited off the misery... it was no wonder he would think I would be delighted by this. What omega wouldn't be? Especially one in my situation. After all, I'd thought I would be dead by the end of this day. Instead, it seemed, I would be *mated*.

Why the Redwood had fixated on me, I wasn't sure. All I *did* know was that I wanted freedom more than anything, and a big, aggressive alpha wasn't going to give it to me.

I was about to go from one cage to another.

Chapter Six

Coal

I opened my eyes. For a moment, I saw nothing through the blurry haze except white light. There was a soft breeze on my skin and a lovely scent in the air that nearly made me purr with pleasure. A warmth spread through me and utter happiness that I didn't understand.

I lifted my head, breathing in the sweet scent of an omega. *My* omega.

With a gasp, I pushed to my feet, seeking him out. Immediately, I stumbled. The room spun so violently that I had to sit down, then lie down completely, until it stopped.

"It's okay," someone said softly, and my entire being turned into giddy mush. What a sweet voice. Soft mid-tones, a touch of command, and a touch of fear. It seemed to vibrate through him.

I wanted to see him.

Without thinking, I shifted into my human form. With some effort, I managed to roll onto my back.

I caught sight of my omega's figure, lean —*skeletal*, I remembered with a flash—olive skin and dark hair, but before I could see his eyes, or take in any of his features, the room kept moving. And moving.

"Ugh."

My hands gripped the fabric I was lying on, willing everything to stop.

Eventually, I cracked my eyes open, and *finally*, I was able to see him.

My omega was striking, with large, fiery eyes, thick brows and lashes, and dimples that were visible even without a smile. Despite his sweet scent, his gaze was sharp, his lips a tight line, arms crossed where he leaned back against a wall, watching me warily from a distance. He was different from the usual omegas I was exposed to, and even more exquisite.

"Beautiful," I whispered.

The omega blinked slowly but didn't otherwise move.

A hint of anxiety spilled from him, carried on his scent. Unable to read his expression, I tried to sit up. And promptly fell back down, flat on what I now realized was a bed—no. A gurney.

I reached a hand out to the omega.

"Come here."

The omega's gaze fixed to the floor. He didn't move. After a moment, he spoke.

"Do I have a choice?"

I didn't even know what to say for a moment, I was so caught off guard.

"What?" I asked. "Why wouldn't you?"

The omega gave me a long, searching look before *finally* pushing off of the wall. He took the few steps toward me as though walking a plank.

My arm was still extended, eager to feel the other man. He didn't seem to *want* me to touch him... but that didn't make any sense. We were fated, weren't we? The omega had to know it as well as I did. Either way, as he came close enough to reach, the room seemed to dip, and I grabbed on without thinking.

The omega gasped as he was yanked to my side.

I fell flat on my back and for a moment, I lay very still, my arms around my omega's slight waist. I had to squeeze my eyes shut and wait, even though all I wanted was to look at my fated mate, hold him and breathe him in.

"What's wrong with me?" I groaned, eyes still squeezed shut.

"They had to tranquilize you," the omega said. "Remember?"

They? Who were *they*? I could think of nothing past this immediate moment. I waited until everything settled and I could open my eyes again to ask the details, but then my gaze settled on the man I was clinging to and nothing else existed.

A smile lit my face, wonder filling me as my heart swelled.

"I'm Coal Kent," I said. "I'm a fighter for the league."

A smile *almost* touched the omega's lips but faded before it got there.

"I know."

"What's your name?" I asked when he didn't go on.

The omega stared down at me. He was trying hard to control his emotions, but I could sense his shifting scent. Tension, fear, and something else, something like desire, mingled as he stood there in my almost embrace.

He tried to speak, swallowed, and tried again.

"Ember," he managed to say.

That was it? No last name, and no information about who he was. He didn't trust me yet, but it didn't matter.

I would do everything I could to win Ember over. I couldn't imagine what a bait wolf went through. A dark feeling settled over me at the thought. I had walked through those dungeons so many times. I'd known that the bait omegas were kept down there, and I'd chosen to selfishly ignore it. All the while, my own fated mate might have been down there, kept in one of the cells... I pushed the thought away and it wasn't hard with those remarkable eyes there to fall into.

"Ember," I breathed, a smile touching my lips. "I will do everything in the world to win your trust and make you happy."

Ember's eyes widened. He shook his head faintly.

"I—that's not—you don't need to. I don't need anything... I don't *want* anything."

His meaning was clear the moment he said it. He

didn't want to mate with me. Come to think of it, he didn't seem to want anything to do with me.

Very slowly and carefully, I pushed myself up. To my surprise, Ember helped me and even kept a steadying hand on my shoulder while I breathed through the spins. When I finally felt steady enough to face Ember, the omega was biting his lip, worry written all over him.

"Look... they said we have to stay in here until the sedatives wear off. The league president said he would call about my... purchase."

His voice faltered at the word.

My entire whole world was shifting. It was like I was now seeing things from an angle I hadn't even known existed. Deep, visceral empathy filled me for things I'd never thought about before. How could one possibly explain the hurt of being sold, especially when no one had paid to begin with? To the wolves of Lunar City, omegas like Ember—usually kidnapped from low-income neighborhoods—had a worth only to those that stole them. People acted like the omegas themselves held no value to their own lives. Like they were inanimate commodities...

I swallowed, my heart squeezing and bile rising in my throat. Over and over, I'd fought and I'd never even spared a thought for the omega bait wolves that were brought in to antagonize me.

We were so close, only inches between us. I could have leaned in and kissed Ember like I so wanted to. I could have laid him down and given him so much pleasure that he forgot everything else, like how unfair the world was. Instead, I reached out and carefully wrapped my arms around his thin frame, holding him gently, offering him comfort of a different nature, because this moment wasn't about what *I* wanted.

Ember stiffened. He was standing over me but after a moment, he sagged the slightest bit, and I took that as a victory.

I knew that a protective alpha's scent could make an omega relax, so I kept Ember close and stroked his back, my own gaze drooping in bliss from being so near him. He just smelled so *good*.

I turned my face, pressing into Ember's neck, which happened to be at just the right level, a happy accident.

A soft moan left my lips, and Ember stilled but didn't pull away.

This, I was sure, was a miracle. From being a man content in my loneliness, someone often called cold and aggressive, to *this*. I was somehow one of the lucky few. I was with my mate.

"How did this happen?" I breathed.

I could feel Ember's heart racing in the pulse point on his neck, just under his scent gland, exactly where I could so easily sink my teeth into the flesh and claim Ember for good. Make it official so that everyone knew. I was filled with a possessiveness I had never felt before. A desire to hold Ember in my arms and fight anyone who even looked at him. Even the thought of other alphas seeing Ember, let alone *touching* him made my pheromones pump, exuding my dominance. A bite, a *knot*, would fix that because then no one could argue that Ember belonged with me. They would smell me on him. That thought was breathtaking.

"They shot you with a sedative," Ember was saying, voice tinged with worry, a hint of fear slipping from his scent gland. Why? From the memory?

"You said that," I said, frowning. "Who did? Why?"

Suddenly, the extent of my fogginess became clear. My head felt like it was held under water, and my brain was sluggish.

"The league security did because you went... well, *feral*..."

He didn't seem to want to say it. The scent of his fear intensified and finally, I realized that fear was directed toward me.

"I would *never* hurt you!" I snarled.

Ember flinched, his entire body stiffening. The fact that I had said it so passionately probably wasn't wise with an omega already seemingly terrified of me for whatever reason. The smell of his fear, now swamping the room, was making me feel sick, but suddenly, I couldn't dwell on it because other things were coming to mind.

The league tranquilized me. They only tranquilized alphas who lost control. I never did, not entirely... Except, I couldn't remember what had happened.

A flash of images returned to me; my first moment seeing Ember, Lambert cowering back, lights flashing, *blood*, Ember trying to get away from me and the fierce protective fear that someone else might get him, *no one could touch him, he was mine, mine, mine!*

I stood. The floor dipped, and Ember stumbled back, all the way until his back hit the wall again.

"Please," he whispered.

What he was begging for, I wasn't sure. *Surely*, he wasn't afraid that I would hurt him. I wouldn't. I protected those that were mine. I would die before letting anything bad ever happen to them.

Asha.

Stunned, I stood very still as yet more memories returned to me. The full extent of what had happened hit me with a staggering force.

I'd found my fated mate and my beast had chosen him over my own sister.

I didn't know where she was. I didn't know what had happened to her.

I didn't know how to fix this.

Chapter Seven

Ember

The alpha paced the room in agitation, fury pouring out of him, stinking up the room until I felt nauseated.

For a minute there, when the alpha had been holding onto me, his scent had felt so comforting, so warm and almost loving, that I had nearly forgotten that this man was a beast. I'd watched the guy kill— or nearly kill, I wasn't sure—his opponent, and then I'd been locked in a room with him. A defenseless omega with a raging alpha. It was wrong. But no one regarded street omegas as anything other than a quick fix to a rut. A means to an end. It was sickening.

If I'd had any sort of status in society, or any alphas in my family to protect me, my entire life would have been different. But again, I was reminded that I had to watch out for myself because no one else would.

Case in point, I was currently cowering against the wall, eyes trained on the alpha, whom I could only think of in that term. He raged, pulling at his hair, hitting the walls when he reached them with bare fists. His hands were shaking. Every now and then, the claws protruded, and he would look at me, grimace, and force them back in. The fact that he was stumbling from the sedative's effects didn't help matters. I didn't know which way he would go next, which direction he would fall. Every time he came near me, my entire body stiffened. Ready for any sudden movements.

For the millionth time, my gaze darted to the window.

I'd checked it the instant we had been locked in this room alone, ready to try my second attempted escape through a window again, but we were three stories up.

Would I survive if I jumped to the street below?

Unlikely, but still, I considered it. Better to jump than end up on the other side of those long, sharp claws, right?

"Phone, phone, phone," the alpha was muttering. "Where is my fucking phone?"

Assuming he could only be talking to me, I answered, my voice betraying me with a tremble.

"I don't know, Alpha," I said.

When the alpha swung around to face me, my gaze dropped hastily to the carpet. How ironic that I was finally given a comfortable room to stay in, but I had to share it with a beast.

"Coal," he snarled. "My name is *Coal* and I told you I wouldn't hurt you. I would *never* hurt you. I'll kill anyone who touches you."

And there it was again, the almost sweet declaration that swiftly turned possessive and violent. The cliche alpha.

I nodded submissively, still avoiding meeting the alpha's gaze.

"Yes, Alpha—Coal."

I bit my lip, fear spiking. Any moment now, if I said or did the wrong thing... would the alpha do something to punish me? He sure as hell seemed like the type, yet somewhere deep inside, I didn't believe it. I was afraid, yes, because Coal was erratic and not in his right mind—when had he been, really? Yet I couldn't deny that in all the time since we had first seen each other, Coal had been more concerned with keeping others away from me than hurting me.

I remembered the way his arm had felt wrapped around my waist, how safe I had felt for a moment there. It was hard to even believe now, minutes later with Coal like this.

"Right," he suddenly muttered. "We're leaving."

I looked up at Coal as he marched toward me and offered a hand to help me up as though there was no arguing, which, I supposed, was the truth.

In human form, Coal was nearly as intimidating as he was as a wolf. He was tall, broad-shouldered and muscular with thick black hair that was cropped short, a soft-looking black beard, and pale, piercing eyes. I knew why he was called the Redwood now; because he seemed sturdy as a tree and like nothing could knock him or best him.

I reached my hand up.

Coal took it at once and the strangest thing happened: his gaze softened, and his shoulders seemed to sag, tension leaving them.

He pulled me gently to my feet but didn't release me, holding my hand in his large, warm grip, thumb stroking my knuckles.

"I'm sorry I frightened you," he said, and I knew he meant it. I could feel the emotion, almost like it was my own—a pang of regret.

Finally, the reality of my situation dawned on me. It was said that fated mates could feel each other to a degree that no one else understood, that they knew what the other was feeling and sometimes even what they were thinking. With the adrenaline of the fight and then the drugs coursing through Coal's body, I hadn't felt it, not until now.

As I gazed into Coal's surprisingly gentle eyes, panic nearly overwhelmed me.

Coal reached out at once, frowning. He held my cheek, fingers sliding into my long, dark hair.

"It's okay," he said, and his words coupled with his nearness calmed me. Especially when he pulled me closer and pressed my face against his scent gland. Despite myself, my eyes rolled and I sagged into him.

Coal caught me, holding me firmly yet gently and I couldn't remember *ever* feeling so safe, so protected.

In all my years, rushed couplings with other alphas or even the gentle care of my older brother had never made me feel so... *good*.

I inhaled and had to bite back a moan. What was

wrong with me? I was stronger than this. I wasn't just an omega cliche, at the very least. I never had been before, but at this moment, I didn't *want* to pull myself away.

"Better?" Coal breathed softly into my hair.

I swallowed and physically forced myself to pull back. I managed a nod, unable to meet my alpha's gaze—no, not *my*, not yet.

I blinked. *Not yet?*

"What's happening to me?" I muttered.

Coal stroked back my hair, and my body betrayed me further by leaning into the touch.

"It's natural for your alpha to calm you," he said, a surprising gentleness in his voice.

There was that sentiment again.

"You're not mine," I pointed out.

Coal's eyes darkened, his gaze dropping to my neck, exactly where a mating mark would go.

"*I am.* But don't worry, we'll make it official."

I wanted to point out that I wasn't worried. That, in fact, I wanted to get away and live life on my own terms. At the very least, I hoped to not to be sent back into that dark cellar where I had been kept for so long now.

Unfortunately for me though, I couldn't deny

that Coal's words soothed something inside me, and I realized that I had soothed Coal right back.

He was steadier now, holding me in his arms like I belonged there. The anger that had been emanating from him was now a hum in the background, a pressing feeling not to be ignored, but no longer an overwhelming force.

With a reluctant sigh, Coal pulled back.

"Time to go."

"They want us to wait here," I reminded him. "They're going to let you buy me... if that's what you want."

The idea itself had stung, the fact that I was going to be used to make money for the people who had almost killed me, the fact that I had no say in who took me. The only consolation, of course, had been that if I was taken out of this place, I might actually stand a chance of escaping.

Coal was frowning at me, as though I'd said something perplexing.

"Did I not make it clear enough?" Before I could answer, Coal leaned closer, lips brushing my ear. "I want you. Of course I do, but they can't sell you when you don't belong to them. You are *mine*... and I am yours."

He leaned down and suddenly pressed his face into my scent gland.

It took me a moment to realize what Coal was doing. He was *scenting* me, dousing me with his own pheromones.

A mark of ownership.

A shiver traveled down my spine as his pheromones overwhelmed my senses. It was dizzying and comforting, like he could make me fall but would just as easily catch me.

Finally, Coal pulled back, meeting my eyes.

"Understood?" he asked, voice low and gravelly.

I managed a dazed nod.

Pleased, Coal pressed our cheeks together and took a deep breath, openly inhaling my new scent.

"And as for that other matter, I am not staying here and letting them use my family as pawns any longer. It's time to take matters into my own hands."

I had no clue what he was talking about. No explanation was given either. Instead, Coal went to the locked door and, standing back a few feet, took a deep steadying breath and then ran full tilt into it. With a deafening *bang*, it smashed off the hinges, wood and dust splintering around him like a cloud.

I stared as the dust settled.

There were two betas at the door, guarding it,

but when they saw Coal standing there, the broken door spread around him, they stood back.

Coal reached for me, not looking to see if I would come, if I would obey. Expecting me to listen.

I did, but partially because my wish was being granted. I was getting the fuck out of this hellhole, and I was going to walk out the front door. No running or climbing through windows.

Coal gripped my hand almost too tightly and led me into the hall. He was glowering at the guards, and I realized the only reason they weren't being attacked was because they weren't alphas and Coal's scent was already all over me as a warning.

"Your phone," he growled, holding his hand out to one of them.

The beta handed it over, stepping hastily back when Coal's chest immediately rumbled with a growl.

The moment the beta was back far enough, Coal began to pull me through the halls.

How were we going to get anywhere like this? How, when he couldn't stand anyone coming too close to me?

The things Coal had said appealed to me on a base level. My omega instincts yearned for a companion, for protection and safety, yet my stomach twisted with unease because I *wasn't* a typical omega.

I was a street rat. I'd been on my own for most of my life. I knew how to take care of myself. Coal's statement of ownership rang in my ears, but the alpha hadn't mated me on the spot. For whatever reason, he hadn't forced me to take his bite yet. Probably wanted to get me to his home first, where we wouldn't be disturbed and where I would be confined in a different way.

I'd seen them all my life, the omegas so controlled by pheromones that they weren't even themselves anymore. They were nothing but glorified slaves, baby-makers and little more with no autonomy and no freedom. I'd always rebelled against becoming that and now, after being imprisoned, my freedom meant even more to me than ever.

Coal pulled me through a door and, suddenly, we were in the front entryway. My breath caught, because I'd never seen it before and it looked so normal. A big open space, an information desk. High glass ceiling and beautiful dark wood floors. I could imagine all the people arriving, looking respectable and clean and expensive. Ready to watch the bloodshed.

We stepped through the large front doors, onto

the street in front of the stadium. It was late at night. There was no one around, just a vast empty street lit by neon lights. The sign for the fight stadium glowed above us.

And just like that, I was free.

Sort of.

I looked at Coal. The alpha immediately caught my eye, flashing a smile.

I wanted to run, to dance and shout and laugh. I'd thought I was going to die, but instead, I was alive and I was out! I almost felt like I might cry.

Coal's scent, his confident speech about us owning each other, it had been good. It had nearly reeled me in, but the facts were, whether we really were fated or not, I would not sacrifice my life to being an alpha's toy.

I needed a bit of time. Some food, rest, and a plan and then I was leaving. I'd hide so well, no one could ever take me again.

Chapter Eight

Coal

I was at a crossroads. On the one hand, I had my mate at my side. On the other, Asha was missing. If I went after her—I *couldn't* leave Ember alone, not until we were mated properly. But if I took the time for that, who knew what the bastards would do to Asha in the meantime? It felt like my heart was being torn in two.

I pulled the phone up, wondering who to call first for a moment, but Ember's small, warm hand in my own made my decision for me. I had to get him home, in my own space where he would be safe.

I dialed Everest's number, waiting impatiently while it rang. Cursing, I dialed again.

This time, the call was answered.

"Ever, it's me."

"Oh, thank god," the other alpha exhaled. "I was worried as hell. No one would say where they took you. Are you okay?"

"They had me locked up in a room to recover and discuss business."

And probably to mate my omega too. I would be safer then, more amenable to whatever they wanted.

"Shit," Everest muttered.

"Can you come get us?"

"You're at the club? I'll be there in fifteen minutes."

I hung up and turned to Ember.

He was clinging to my hand, shifting back and forth on his bare feet. The ground was cold, I realized. I'd been so caught up in the moment, I'd barely registered it.

"Come here," I said, steering Ember back toward the building. I just wanted to stand inside the doors but as soon as Ember realized where he was being taken, he dug his heels in and those unusual eyes turned up to me in a suspicious gaze.

"What are you doing?" he demanded.

"It's warmer inside the door," I said, stung despite myself that Ember didn't trust me.

"I'd rather wait right here."

There was a challenge in Ember's voice and his eyes like he was expecting me to drag him in there and prove—what exactly, I wasn't sure.

"Okay," I said after a moment.

Ember blinked, surprised, and my confusion grew. It was as if the omega expected me to disregard his wishes, to force him to do as he was told... I supposed that was what he was used to.

My grip tightened on Ember's hand and without thinking, I pulled him closer, wrapping my arms around him.

Ember was still in the thin clothes he'd entered the fight in. Wearing only my fight shorts, I was in even less.

With so little between us, heat traveled fast, warming us straight through.

Ember felt so lovely in my arms, so perfect, so sexy. I took a slow breath, burying my face into his dark curls and everything felt *right*. A moan drifted from my lips, my cock hardening. Against my thigh, I felt Ember's body reacting in a similar fashion.

We were right on the side of the street but suddenly, I couldn't take it anymore. I wanted

Ember, wanted to bury myself deep inside him, to sink my teeth into his flesh, to become one. But we couldn't do this right here.

My gaze drifted to the alley nearby and the shameful realization that I had indeed fucked an omega there once, after a fight, hit me. I didn't know their name, barely even remembered a face. Ember deserved better. He deserved to be on his back on my soft bedding, comfortable enough that he'd be able to take it all night because that was how I was going to do it. I would take my time, devour every inch of my mate, his cock and his hole, yes, but I would lick and touch every bit of his skin right to his toes and take it so slow that Ember begged for me.

A low groan left my lips, and Ember's hands, which had settled on my hips, clenched, his body shuddering as though he could hear my thoughts.

The sudden loud *honk* from a car next to us made Ember jump. I tightened my hold, somewhat disappointed, and looked over at Everest who was leaning out the driver's side window with a grin.

"This was basically the scene I expected to stumble upon," he said.

I couldn't return the smile. My heart nearly stopped with the realization that I was going to lock my unmated omega in a car with another alpha. I would be there too, but...

Everest took in my expression, seeing the way I shifted to put Ember behind me, despite my logical brain knowing that Everest wouldn't come near him.

He sat back into his car, worry clouding his expression.

"Shit," Everest muttered, "you didn't mate him? What the hell were you thinking?"

"There was no time," I growled. "*Asha...*"

Everest grimaced.

"They took her away while we were distracted by the disaster that was you finding your mate mid-fight."

"I have to get her back."

Everest nodded.

"I know, but it's the middle of the night. We don't even know where she is."

I swallowed, fear enveloping me, momentarily pushing everything else away.

A hand landed on my shoulder from behind. Ember was trying to comfort me. It warmed me straight through, and some of the fear softened.

"Look, just get in the car," Everest said. "I'll speed you home."

I squeezed my eyes shut, unsure if I could.

Everest was my friend, I reminded myself. He'd always been loyal and easygoing. He wasn't the type to force anyone or fight outside of the ring.

Taking a deep breath, I nodded, but when it came to it, it was a bit harder than that.

I pressed Ember into the corner of the back seat, as far from Everest as possible, and my entire body tightened with aggression. My gaze fixed on Everest. Any wrong move and I would kill him.

As he pulled away from the curb, Everest kept shooting me glances in the mirror, worry etched in the lines between his brows.

An unending growl rumbled in my chest, growing louder every time our gazes caught. The longer we were confined within, the more the car swung wildly, Everest losing his cool and probably running every light. I wasn't sure because I couldn't look away from the mirror.

Finally, Everest turned the car into the driveway and pulled over so fast we nearly got whiplash. He threw open the driver's door and leaped from his seat.

The sudden movement made me act. I lunged forward, claws extended, *just* missing Everest as he got outside. He paced in a wide circle, letting out a shout.

"Fuck!"

He paused at a distance to bend and look in the window while I forced my claws back in and tried to breathe and calm down.

"Coal, you are *so* lucky that your bestie is a saint! Not many people would get in a car with you right now."

That was probably true.

I turned my gaze to Ember.

He was sitting very silently in his corner, keeping himself small and unthreatening. He deferred his gaze when I looked at him, but there was no fear in his scent. He knew how to handle alphas, clearly.

That thought made me uneasy, but I pushed it away.

"Welcome home," I said instead and pushed the door open for him to step out first. I followed closely, still worried that Everest might make a move for him.

He didn't. He stayed where he was on the opposite side of the car.

Still, I glowered at him in warning, backing Ember toward my house without letting Everest out of my sight.

He rolled his eyes.

"Call me in the morning when you're normal again."

I managed a curt nod and opened the door without taking my eyes off him.

Once Ember was over the threshold, I followed him closely and shut the door behind us. Finally, I could breathe.

Chapter Nine

Ember

The house was dark. Silent. I didn't need to be told that we were the only ones here.

Alone with Coal, my nerves spiked.

Being near him was like being wrapped in insulation: warm, comfortable, and *itchy*. I couldn't help wanting to put distance between us while, at the same time, I soaked in the warmth of being near him. I was confused. And I was scared.

A light flicked on, illuminating an entryway far nicer than I had been expecting. The floor was polished marble, the ceilings high with a dim chandelier hanging from above.

Right. Coal was the current champion. I couldn't even imagine what level of payment he got for each fight he won. Probably millions.

A large hand landed on my back, not pushing me or steering me, just letting me know it was there.

I looked at Coal's face, at his rough, masculine features that were unexpectedly beautiful.

"What would you like first?" Coal asked. "Food? Rest? Something else?"

I purposely ignored the last suggestion, my stomach dipping at the heated look in Coal's eyes as he said it.

"Food," I murmured.

Coal nodded, motioning for me to follow him. He looked back after a few steps, making sure I was nearby. That almost made me laugh. Truth be told, I didn't have the strength to fight our connection right now. My body moved of its own accord, closer to Coal's back than I had been planning, and then, despite myself, I inhaled the alpha's scent as subtly as I could.

A calmness immediately settled over me.

I was led to a large living room. A lamp was on in the corner, casting shadows across the walls from the large, plush couch, the wrought iron tables, and the I.

To my surprise, a mat made up of the letters of the alphabet was tucked against one corner. A child-sized desk and chair sat atop it, as well as a storage box overflowing with toys. Pictures clearly painted by a child were hung up on the wall.

I turned to Coal, eyes wide, but the alpha didn't notice what I was looking at because he was already leaving the room.

"Make yourself comfortable," he said. "I'll just be a minute."

For the first time since the fight, Coal left me.

For a minute, I was dumbfounded. Then I heard Coal's mumbled voice and realized that he hadn't gone far. He had shut the door to the next room, but he was just on the other side of it, clearly not willing to leave too much space between him and his new omega.

I could hear the worried tone of his voice, then the clipped edges, then, worst of all, *defeat*.

I wanted to help him. It was so weird.

I didn't know Coal, and yet I wanted to open the door between us and do *something* to make him feel better. Whatever the issue was, suddenly, I thought I could fix it.

Was this how every mated omega felt? *Poor bastards...* It was unbearable.

Coal's voice lowered, growing distant, and I realized he was walking away.

If I really wanted to run, now was probably the time, but that couch looked awfully comfortable and inviting.

Giving in, I went to it, lowering onto the velvety fabric and nearly moaning in pleasure.

I couldn't remember anything quite so comfortable.

Despite myself, I laid back, stretching out aching muscles.

This room was bigger than the hotel room I had rented for years before I was taken. The Belfort Hotel was in the worst area of town and known for being a shithole. The rooms and facilities had rarely been cleaned and there were cockroaches in the bathrooms, but, for a while, it had been home.

I used to roll my eyes at the wealthy shifters. There were enough aristocrats in the city that I'd grown a dislike for the upper crust of society, the types who would cover their noses if I passed. I knew that often I probably needed a shower, but could they really smell me from feet away? To even be *invited* into a house like this... to potentially mate with someone who *owned* a house like this... I wasn't sure how I felt about it. Except a touch of excitement filled me, images accosting me at once of warm, clean clothes, soft bedding, hot water... My mouth was watering.

Maybe it wouldn't be so bad for a little while. Just until I could make it on my own again.

In the car, we had both calmed down from that heated embrace. Coal had been too distracted by the other alpha to pay me much attention, which I understood. Alphas had issues with other alphas around their omegas, especially when they hadn't mated yet. He wanted me, that much was obvious and made even more so as we had stood embracing on the chilly street. Coal's hard length had sent a thrill through my entire being—and remembering it now was affecting my body again.

With a groan, I pushed the thought away. I wasn't going to live up to the cliche of the sex-obsessed omega. That stereotype had put me in enough shit situations in my life that I actively rebelled against it.

I squeezed my eyes shut, and my exhausted body, finally finding some reprieve, almost immediately drifted to sleep.

Chapter Ten

Coal

I dug my claws into the palms of my hands. Just enough pain to keep me grounded.

"Do you know how much you cost us with that little stunt of yours?" Alek's snarl through the line set my teeth on edge, fangs itching to cut free.

"It wasn't a stunt," I gritted out. "I was planning to lose the fight like we agreed, then the club brought in my omega."

"You want me to believe you lost it for cheap bait omega." His laugh burst down the line, grating on all of my senses.

"Not a cheap bait omega." The words burned my throat. "*My* omega. Get it? My fated mate."

Silence rang through the line, and I went on.

"I couldn't control myself. I don't even remember what happened."

When the silence continued, I forced my voice lower. I wouldn't beg, but I would ask nicely, at the very least.

"Give me another chance. Just give me my sister today, and I promise I'll do anything you ask."

The continued silence made my heart pound. Finally, Alek let out a heavy sigh.

"Look, I'm not in the habit of killing kids and now we're stuck with the girl. It's lose-lose, really."

His words didn't comfort me. Killing was only one of the many terrible things that could be done to a small child.

"So you'll bring her to me?"

Alek snorted.

"I didn't say that. But tell you what, you give us the money we lost on you, and you'll get her back right then."

My hands were shaking. Rage coursed through me.

I had money. I could do it, but how was I now

the one to owe them? It didn't seem very fair. Then again, when did gangsters play by the rules?

"How much?"

"Get us fifty million and we'll call it even."

My eyes widened. Okay, I didn't have *that* much, but I schooled my voice, mind racing with options.

"By... let's say Monday," he added.

"Deal. Keep her safe and I'll be in touch as soon as possible with the money."

Without waiting for a response, I hung up. My body felt heavy, defeated.

How was I going to come up with that? Maybe if I called in every favor I could, took out loans with every bank, and sold my house...

I groaned. Even if I could get that much, it would take a couple of days, at least.

I looked at the large clock hung up on the wall. It was past one A.M., and my omega was hungry.

I would grab us both something to eat and then... My body heated at the possibilities.

We should really get some sleep. It was going to be a long day tomorrow, but I wasn't going to turn Ember away if he was in the mood to give me what I wanted.

Sighing, I went to the kitchen, rifling through the fridge. I hadn't had dinner but with the worry eating me up inside, my appetite wasn't there. Instead of making something elaborate, I grabbed crackers, hummus, and some veg and went back to the living room.

"Sorry about that—"

I fell silent when I caught sight of Ember, stretched out on the couch, fast asleep.

Quietly, I set the plate of food down on one of the tables and walked up to him.

For the first time, with no pressing issues at hand, I felt like I could just look at him.

His hair was spread out around him, dark curls tangled and dull. His face was gaunt, the shape of his skull far too visible through thin skin. But in sleep, the ever-present line between Ember's brows smoothed out and he looked peaceful and undeniably beautiful in a way that made my chest ache. Like a glass figurine. Breakable.

I knelt down at his side, watching him for a moment longer. Finally, as carefully as I could, I slid my arms under Ember, adjusting him so that his head landed on my shoulder.

He must have been exhausted because he didn't so much as twitch when I lifted him. My breath caught because he was so light it was scary.

My heart twisted once again, thinking of Ember

being kept somewhere in the fight league's under-belly. How long had he been there? How were the bait wolves treated? Had they bothered to feed him at all?

Tomorrow, I would ask him about it, but for now, we both needed to sleep.

I carried Ember up to my bedroom, stretching him out on the sheets and covering him with the blanket before crawling into bed next to him.

I lay next to him, able to see his form in the soft light from the nightlight I always left on for Asha in case she had a nightmare and wanted to sleep with me in the middle of the night.

My gaze raked the line of his profile. He may as well have been a constellation in the sky. That was how weird it felt to have him here. This stranger who wasn't one. My soulmate.

I was so tired, but how could I sleep? Everything that had happened today left me feeling whiplash.

Then there was the fact that Ember lying next to me, his body so warm, his sweet scent soaking into my pillows, was pretty much a recipe for an aching hard-on. I ignored it as best I could, but couldn't resist engulfing Ember in my arms and breathing him in.

Once again, holding him seemed to ease all the

fears in my heart. Alek had suggested that he wouldn't hurt Asha and she had seemed quite happy when I'd seen her briefly at the fight.

If she escaped from this with *any* trauma, we would have to deal with it then. Surely no one would be stupid enough to hurt her, right? They must have known that I would rest at nothing to end anyone who so much as broke a strand of the pretty brown hair on her head.

Sighing, I pushed the thoughts away. I could take at least a few hours of sleep before tackling this with a fresh head.

With a soft sigh, Ember suddenly rolled in toward me, his arm going around my waist as he nuzzled in closer. My heart melted, my body relaxed, and sleep overtook me.

* * *

I was swiftly brought to consciousness by the feeling of arms squeezing my waist tightly, and a hard cock digging into my thigh. A heady moan and thick aroused omega pheromones nearly brought me to the edge of an orgasm before I'd fully opened my eyes.

I gasped, sluggish brain catching up to what was

happening as I rolled Ember under me, pressing my weight down on him, dragging our cocks together.

Ember groaned, his head falling back, exposing his bare neck.

Morning light was filtering through the window, illuminating the room enough that I could see his flushed cheeks and the way his chest quickly rose and fell.

"Fuck," he breathed, and his eyes fluttered open, glimmering gaze fixing on mine. "I need you."

I didn't need any more encouragement than that. I reached between us, gripped the edges of Ember's thin pants, and tore the fabric apart, exposing his hard cock, already wet with precome. My own cock throbbed for release, and he gripped my shorts, shoving them down.

I was desperate to fuck my mate and make our bond official.

And I was so swept up in arousal that I nearly did just that. I almost thrust into him without any warning. At the last moment though, my thoughts caught up and I stopped myself. I stilled, taking a deep breath of air soaked with the scent of our desire, and lowered myself down his body.

I was too far gone to be anything but clumsy when I took Ember's length into my mouth. He was bigger than most omegas, his shaft long and straight and so fucking delicious. My hand slipped lower, feeling his already-slick entrance before pressing a finger into it.

Ember cried out, his hands gripping my hair unforgivingly.

I groaned around his length, bobbing all but twice, my hand moving with me, thrusting into Ember's hole before his grip clenched even tighter and he came with a deep moan that shot straight into my gut like hot fire, making me impossibly harder as his sweet liquid burst into my mouth.

I stilled as Ember shuddered into me, enjoying the blissful moment and the temporary release of precome that spurted from my tip.

When I finally lifted my head, Ember was lying loosely back on the pillows, his chest and face flushed, his body pliant.

I climbed up to him and brushed our lips together softly before pressing him down, deepening the kiss.

When I took Ember's thighs in my hands, the omega's legs parted for me eagerly with no hesitation or fear. He'd obviously done this before.

The unfortunately timed thought did something to me.

Oppressive, possessive anger coursed through me.

"What's wrong?" Ember gasped, breaking our kiss at once.

My cock was edging his dripping wet hole, both of our bodies ready and willing, and I was thinking of other alphas fucking my own.

I wouldn't ruin this moment, I decided. We could talk about our pasts later if we needed to.

I shut my eyes, pressed our foreheads together, and sighed.

"Just an intrusive thought," I said and pushed inside him.

We both groaned and everything else was forgotten as I pressed as deep as I could into my partner's slick warmth.

Ember couldn't quite take me all the way. He was too tight. His grip tightened around me, his body stiff even though he was keening softly with each movement. I sympathized. His hot heat, clinging tightly to my cock, was blissfully unbearable as I thrust into him.

I pressed my face into his neck, breathing him in as I fucked him slowly, his scent heightening the pleasure as I carefully stretched him open. After a minute fucking him, he could finally take my entire length.

I groaned as I bottomed out and ground my cock in, twisting my hips until Ember started to shake with pleasure, soft cries leaving his lips with every push.

It was so good. Better than anything I'd ever felt before because this was more than just a fuck. I could feel it deeper than just my physical body. My very spirit seemed to sing as we came together.

In the midst of something dark in my life, I'd somehow been given *this*.

My lips parted instinctively, teeth sinking into Ember's flesh.

Ember cried out in pleasure as my entire body was consumed by it.

I came harder than I could ever remember, hands digging into the sheets, cock straining inside Ember as I unloaded deep inside him.

When I finally came down, I realized my teeth were still clamped down, embedded in his flesh.

I had to physically force my jaw to relax and unlatch from Ember's shoulder. Blood gushed free as I released him, tainting the air with the metallic scent. I ran my tongue over the broken, bleeding flesh, instinctively.

Ember shivered and my arms tightened around him. I could feel my knot swelling and hesitated, wondering if I should pull out or if Ember would mind if I stayed right where I was. I never had before. Normally sex was a means to an end, not an opportunity to stay close to someone.

When I shifted back the slightest bit to ask, Ember's fingers dug into my back, holding me in place.

"Stay," he whispered. "It feels good."

I sighed, relaxing back down onto my mate. Our bellies were slick with come, but I couldn't care less. Making Ember come twice felt like a victory. A smile lit my face.

"It's official now," I said happily.

Ember chuckled, voice husky from shouting.

"I guess so."

"I didn't expect to wake up to that," I admitted, resting my head on the pillow next to Ember's and turning so I could see the line of his hair just behind his ear.

Ember bit his lip, his eyes drifting shut as I gave in and nuzzled the spot.

"Sleeping next to you was kind of like getting drugged and tortured," Ember breathed. "I was so fucking horny. I could feel you there and my body wanted you, but I couldn't act on it until I started to wake up."

I moaned, pressing my face into Ember's neck now, to the scent gland I'd marked. I breathed him in and my eyes rolled because he smelled like *me* now.

Our pheromones seemed to be interwoven so fully that they were one, my own grounded musk and Ember's soft, light tones. A perfect blend that soothed me deeply.

My inner wolf was happy; I could feel the pleased rumble growing in my chest. A deep satisfaction filled me, an almost blissful euphoria. Ember's scent was tinged by the bit of blood I'd drawn, but I knew it would heal and the mark would take and the whole world would know that we belonged together. He would always carry a hint of my scent, even should anything part us.

I squeezed Ember a little tighter at the thought.

"Does it really feel good?" I asked, giving my hips a little shake, feeling the soft tug at the base of my hard cock as Ember's body gripped my knot.

Ember's breath hitched, eyes rolling shut, and for a minute we were lost again in the pleasure of our bodies, enjoying the sensation of my swollen gland inside him, not yet ready to release.

"I never thought I would have this," I admitted. "I thought it would be just me and Asha forever."

Ember stilled.

"Asha?" he asked. "Your friend mentioned her..."

My chest tightened at the thought of her. In response, Ember's arms squeezed, comforting me.

"Who is she?" he asked. Then, his voice dropping, "Another omega?"

I shook my head, touched by the fact that Ember wanted to comfort me even when he was obviously a little bit jealous.

I lifted my head to look down at him and pressed a kiss to his forehead before answering.

"She's my little sister."

Ember glanced away, perhaps trying to hide the look of relief that fluttered through his eyes.

"What happened to her?"

"Nothing yet... I *think*, anyway."

I took a deep breath and attempted to keep my composure while I explained. I didn't want to get mad again while my mate was currently taking my knot and had nowhere to go should he want some space.

"She was stolen from me for ransom. I was meant to lose that fight to get her back. They put a lot of money on it."

Finally, my member slipped free from Ember's hole as the swelling began to go down. I felt an odd mix of relief and disappointment at that. I didn't want to have this talk while we were stuck together but, at the same time, it just felt so *good*.

Immediately, Ember pushed me back and sat up, peering down at me with a strange look in his eyes.

"You chose me over your own family?" he asked.

Swallowing, I shook my head.

"No," I admitted. I reached for Ember's hand and held it tightly. "I had no control over my actions when I saw you... If I'd been thinking straight, I would have lost the fight and then contacted the league officials about buying you afterward. It would have been great to leave with both you and Asha at my side... Although, I doubt it could have gone any other way. When I saw Lambert in the cage with you, I lost it."

Ember let out a trembling breath.

"What are you going to do?" he asked.

I shrugged helplessly.

"Whatever I have to do to get her back."

Chapter Eleven

Ember

Coal was nothing like I had thought he was. He was the epitome of an alpha, that was true, but he was also kind, caring, and considerate. He had a bigger heart than anyone I had come across in my life—that wasn't saying much, but still, it was refreshing to meet someone who was actually *kind*.

How had I stumbled into this, a mate, a bond, a mark?

It was such an overwhelming change that it seemed too good to be true.

We were sitting in the kitchen. Coal was cooking

me breakfast, his sweats hanging loose on his hips and round ass. I couldn't help staring at his back as he moved, the way his muscles flexed.

Coal turned and, catching me watching, he paused and then sauntered toward me with a pleased smile.

I chuckled, hiding my face before a plate was placed on the table in front of me.

"Does it look good enough to eat?" he asked, and I was pretty sure he wasn't addressing the eggs because he winked.

"Yeah," I said, cheeks heating. "It does."

He smiled, his eyes narrowing in that hungry way that made my mouth dry.

"Eat up," he said.

I nodded, distractedly taking a bite, and immediately, I forgot about the suggestive conversation in favor of another pleasure.

I moaned, devouring each bite.

"Wow," Coal breathed. "I can't wait to see you eating something *actually* good."

I looked up at him, then down at the last of my toast, realizing how quickly I'd torn through it.

"I haven't had a hot meal in months," I said. "This is probably the best thing I've ever eaten."

Sadness filled Coal's eyes, but determination quickly struck out the pitying emotion.

"Then I'll make sure you never have a hungry belly again."

The quiet promise struck a chord and I had to swallow the lump forming in my throat.

Coal reached across the table, placing his hand over mine.

"I mean it," he whispered.

"I know," I choked. "That's what's getting to me."

I blinked back the emotion as best I could.

Alphas had promised me safety before and not one had been able to deliver. Why did Coal make me want to hope?

The doorbell suddenly rang, breaking the moment, but neither of us moved straight away.

"Here," Coal said, sliding his untouched meal to me. "You have mine before it gets cold. I can make more for myself in a minute."

He waited for my nod before getting up to answer.

I managed one bite before the sound of raised voices reached my ears. Instantly, my heart started racing. Fight or flight or freeze hit me at once because this relative peace I currently had was hard-won and it hadn't even been twenty-four hours.

My body tensed as I sat there, unable to move, listening with my weak human ears.

Finally, I stood and crept quietly to the sitting room, peering through the crack left open in the doorway.

I saw the streak of blond hair first and knew immediately who it was. Abram Adair paced the length of Coal's living room, his face blotchy with anger.

"How dare you disrespect me like that?" he snarled.

His voice was clearly threatening, but he wasn't looking at Coal. Clearly, he wouldn't dare challenge him physically. He knew what he was capable of, after all.

"He's my mate." Coal's calm, measured voice left no room for arguing.

From where I stood, I could see only a strip of the bright living room that Abram passed back and forth through. I couldn't see Coal but pride filled me at the control in my mate's tone. I'd thought Coal was hotheaded yesterday, but it seemed that was only because we hadn't bonded yet.

"I don't give a fuck what he is," Abram snapped. "You want one of *my* omegas, you pay."

There was a brief silence and then, "Ember, you can come in."

Abram's eyes widened and he swung around, suddenly meeting my gaze in the doorway.

I swallowed, embarrassed and more than a little uneasy about walking into the middle of this argument.

But somehow, I squared my shoulders and walked in. I pretended I didn't notice the way Abram's gaze went over the huge shirt and pants that Coal had given me this morning. They hung right off my thin frame. I'd had to use a belt to hold up the pants and roll them a few times, but it all stayed put and was comfortable, so I couldn't complain. Except that I could see the way Abram was looking me over and could sense his anger growing.

As soon as I was close enough to reach, Coal took my hand and tugged me closer. He was sitting on the armchair and pulled me to sit on the arm, wrapping his thick arm around me like a shield. When our gazes met, Coal offered me a tender smile.

"You hear that?" he asked me. "This guy says that you belong to him. He didn't pay you for rights to your life, did he?"

My lips twitched at the mocking tone. I bit them, managing to keep a straight face, and shook my head.

"Hm, that's strange," Coal mused. "Were you perhaps born in the league's underbelly to Abram's own mate?"

"No," I said, continuing the charade. "I believe I was snatched from my real life, thrown into a pit, and abused for a long time. Certainly not my whole life, but long enough."

Darkness shadowed Coal's playful gray gaze. His arm around me tightened but before he could say anything, Abram growled. Clearly, he'd had enough.

"That'll do," he snarled. "We steal *all* our omegas. That doesn't change the fact that we got him first. You want our omega, then you'll have to pay the same amount everyone else does for them. Get me fifty Gs by Monday or you'll never fight again."

I nearly keeled over just hearing the amount the president wanted for me, but Coal didn't react at all. Not even a twitch.

It didn't make any sense. A day ago, they were willing to let me *die*, so why demand so much money for me now? Supply and demand, I realized. They knew how much Coal wanted me. They could charge what they wanted knowing Coal would pay it.

I swallowed the lump in my throat as Coal pushed to his feet.

"We'll talk more later."

Abram laughed.

"You have the weekend. Get me my money," he said, then turned on his heel and walked from the room, slamming the front door to hard that the room shook.

I looked at Coal, my stomach twisting.

"What are we going to do?" I asked uneasily.

Coal turned, looked at me still perched on the arm of the couch, and pulled me unexpectedly up into his warm, thick arms.

"I guess we'll pay," he said. "It's not right what they did to you. It makes me want to attack him, not reward him... but I can't risk them coming after you again."

I dug my fingers into Coal's side, gripping him tightly just in case my alpha tried to back away.

How do I feel this way?!

In a matter of hours, really, it felt like my entire world had changed. Escape was no longer the cold streets or wilderness on my own. No, now freedom was something else. It was a warm embrace from my mate, the choice for us to do whatever we pleased, *together*. Morning sex and shared showers, maybe dinners out or afternoon walks, movies on the couch with popcorn and chocolate that turned into long make-out sessions. I didn't care. A new, unexpected life was being offered to me and it didn't feel like suppression; it felt like safety and maybe even love, and I didn't want to let it go.

"Hey."

Coal's hands found my cheeks, tilting my head up so that our eyes could meet. Grudgingly, I opened my burning eyes and met my alpha's concerned gaze.

"Don't worry. I won't let them take you."

Relief eased into me, untangling the knots in my stomach.

"I want to stay with you," I admitted.

Coal bent down, a seriousness falling into his eyes as he pressed our foreheads together.

"You're not going anywhere," he whispered. "I promise."

I blinked back those stubborn tears and tilted my head the inch it took for our lips to meet.

It was gratifying that Coal gave in to me. Very quickly it felt like things had changed, like I wanted this at least as much as he did. Then Coal's grip on me changed, pulling me in closer with a heady moan and I felt a bit better about it.

Groaning, Coal wrenched himself away, still

holding me tightly, his hands drifting up and down my sides like he couldn't quite stop himself from touching me.

"I want nothing more than to lay in bed with you all day, but I have to go," he sighed. "I have to contact some people about Asha."

I pushed back my disappointment.

"Of course. Do you know where she is?"

He shook his head.

"No, but Everest and Seymour know someone who might."

A look crossed his face, a grimace of pain.

"I have to get her back, Ember. She's like my daughter, we've never been apart this long."

I was surprised by that. Imagining Coal as a parent made sense though. He was just the type to take a role like that seriously. My heart squeezed at the thought as something else became clear; Coal seemed so... *alone.*

"Do you not have any other family?" I asked gently.

"None that I know of," Coal said. "My mom was killed in an accident years ago, when I was ten."

He swallowed, gaze dropping to the carpet as the memories came and a wave of sadness rolled off him. I held him tightly and waited until he went on.

"My dad was a bit of a degenerate after that, to be honest. Gambling, drinking, drugs, you name it. For his ruts, he would get with street omegas around town... One of them had Asha. She didn't want her. Dropped her on our doorstep when she was born. Of course, my dad didn't want her either, but I did... as soon as I saw her, I knew she was my baby."

He chuckled.

"Good thing I took that attitude from the start too, because a couple months later, Dad vanished. Haven't seen him since."

I grimaced.

"You don't think he's..."

"He might be. His gambling was out of hand. He owed a lot of people. Dead or alive, it doesn't really matter, does it? He stopped being a father a long time ago. That's why my boys are so important to me. My team of fighters are closer than any family I've had."

I didn't know what to say. I felt for this man. I hadn't expected someone living in a house like this to have a past just as dark and unstable as mine had been.

The sudden urge to share *everything* with this person was overwhelming. But we would have time for that later. Right now, for Asha, time was limited, and I now wanted the little girl to be found and brought home more than anything.

I took a deep breath, straightened my shoulders, and pushed Coal back from our embrace.

"Go," I said. "Get her back."

Coal nodded, appreciation in his eyes.

"I won't be long. A couple hours. Will you be here when I get home?"

I nodded, taken aback for a moment. Coal didn't notice though, just swept forward, brushed a kiss to my lips, and left.

I stood there in the big empty house reflecting on everything that had happened in wonder.

I'd found the person I was meant to be with, and he didn't treat me at all like I'd thought he would.

I'd thought I would be controlled. I'd thought he would act as the caged animal he had been in that fight ring. I'd thought I would have no freedom at all.

Still not believing it, I went to the front and back doors, checking if they were locked from the outside.

They both opened.

Coal really trusted me. More than that; he'd given me my freedom *and* his affection.

Maybe this could really work.

Chapter Twelve

Coal

"You normal again?" Everest asked the second I stepped out of my car.

I rolled my eyes.

"I don't have time for your bullshit," I said. "Let's just get this meeting done."

Everest gave me a long look and then laughed.

"Damn, I thought you'd be nicer after you got your mark in the little thing. You *did* fuck him, right?"

"Don't talk about him like that," I growled, and Everest chuckled again.

"Was it good? Life changing? Seymour said it was life changing."

He waited, showing no signs of leading me wherever we were supposed to go, and finally, I caved.

"The best ever," I sighed.

Everest whooped.

"So, the stories are true? How do you feel? Are you a new person? Is it unbearable being apart? Is your soul whole again?"

He had tears in his eyes because apparently mocking my newfound happiness was really *that* funny.

"All one hundred percent correct," I agreed, not cracking a smile. "The only thing ruining it is not having my daughter with me."

Everest grimaced, finally pulling his grin back.

"Sorry, sorry. Let's go get her."

He patted me on the shoulder as he led me down the street.

In many ways, the business district of Lunar City known as Shadow Alley to locals was just as shady as the name implied.

Skyscrapers towered over us, blotting out the morning sun as Everest led me from our meeting point at a nearby intersection and onto a smaller side street where the buildings didn't reach as high.

The streets here were clean and broad, nothing like the scene in "the valley," as it was called. It was the roughest, most degenerate part of the city, sand-wiched between the high-scale businesses of Shadow Alley and the penthouses that overlooked the water on the other side.

For new visitors to Lunar City, the juxtaposition of the absolute edges of society only a block from the immense wealth of the upper class was hard to come to terms with.

Having lived here my whole life though, I didn't even bat an eye at the quick decline in the neighbor-hood as we walked toward the valley.

Even the crowd began to change from the upright businessmen of Shadow Alley. Beggars sat in the doorways of the businesses here and those unlucky enough to work on this street had to step over them to get inside.

I caught sight of Seymour standing at the doorway to one somewhat rundown building. His large form was hard to miss.

Like all of the fighters on our team, he was a big guy and not just in stature. He was muscular too and had a right hook that could take out anyone.

Until he'd found his mate, he'd been unstoppable

in the ring. Now, he mostly held pads for the rest of us while we trained.

I could sympathize. Finding your mate changed your perspective on things. In one night, I already had a lot to think about.

But all of that would have to wait until later.

"Hey buddy," Everest said, clapping hands with Seymour as we reached him.

"How are you?" he asked, hitting my shoulder in greeting. He said it casually, but his sharp gaze looked straight through me.

I shrugged and that seemed to say it all.

"Alright. Let's go see my guy," he said, holding the door open for us.

We entered the shabby, carpeted lobby, which smelled mildly of mold, and went straight to the elevator.

"It's a weird one," Everest said to me once we were moving. "I want to tease you and get all the juicy details about your new mate, but then there's Asha's kidnapping putting a damper on the situation."

Seymour huffed.

"How come you never asked about me and Glen?" he demanded.

"Because I don't give a fuck about you," Everest joked.

They pretended to glare at each other for a moment before the faked heat faded. What was left in their eyes in the exchanged gaze spoke volumes.

They always were close. Had grown up together and everything. As far as I could tell, they were basically brothers at this point. Nothing would get in between them.

"Really though," Seymour said, "how are you two? It must be tough dealing with this shit while you have your new mate waiting for you at home."

"I think he's happy to be with me now that we've spent some time together," I admitted. "I really didn't want to leave his side... It's been a bit overwhelming."

Seymour patted my shoulder as the elevator door opened.

"Well, let's see if Mr. P.I. can't fix things for us."

I didn't like the fact that I was ready to hire someone. The money spent on this P.I. could be put toward paying for Asha and Ember, but when I really thought about it, I would be damned if I gave those gangsters a cent. Asha was mine. They stole her. As far as I was concerned, they'd be lucky to receive anything other than a beating. The same went for Ember. They didn't deserve to get paid for the hell they had put him through.

Jaw set, I followed them down a narrow corridor until we slowed to a stop in front of a thick wooden door.

Alistair Alvy P.I. was the name etched into the plaque.

The man himself, when the secretary let us into his office, turned out to be a beta of medium build with medium brown hair and a plain face. He wore glasses and a suit that looked like it was well-loved based on the threads hanging at the wrists. He didn't look very impressive, but maybe that was the point.

"I'll find her," he said as soon as I explained the situation. "I have no doubt of that."

His confidence sent a buzz of hope through my chest.

"How soon?" I asked.

"Can't say for sure," Alvy said, "but probably a couple of days, max. I've been keeping tabs on the Belkin brothers on and off for other clients. I know their habits and where to start watching from."

He checked his watch.

"I can start today. They'll be at their usual haunt for a Saturday. All I'll need is a down payment and the papers filled."

Part of me couldn't believe it *could* be that easy, but Everest gave me an excited thumbs up, and Seymour seemed to really trust the guy or he wouldn't have brought me here.

I nodded.

"Deal."

Alvy pulled out a questionnaire and went through the details with me: what Asha looked like, what she was wearing the last time I'd seen her, and any other information I had. I told him about how they had taken her around town and let her watch movies. Just because it didn't seem like she was having a bad time, didn't change anything. I was angry and scared to have her out of my sight.

"And when I find her, what would you like me to do? Alert the authorities?"

I shook my head at once.

"No. Just let me know the second you find out. I'll go get her, and I'll deal with the assholes keeping her with my own two hands." And my claws, my fangs. I would destroy them and leave whatever shreds remained of their bodies as a warning to the rest of the gangsters.

Everest's hand landed on my shoulder, comforting me.

"Alright, I'll be in touch soon with any updates."

When we stood to leave, I reached out and shook the detective's hand.

"Thank you," I said.

My world was out of alignment, but if Asha could be brought home and if I could come to some kind of stalemate with the gangsters then there would only be one other matter to deal with. Ember's freedom from the fight league.

It was so frustrating. I felt like I was on the cusp of true contentment, balancing on the edge, unable to let go without everything falling apart.

I had to fix this. I had to keep my family safe.

"What's on your mind?" Everest asked as we walked to our cars. "You stink of anxiety."

"I need to fix this," I said, echoing my thoughts.

Everest nodded.

"You will, and I'll be by your side helping."

"We all will," Seymour said. "The entire gang will be there if you need. We could scour the streets and break down doors that might be hiding her. Just say the word."

I paused as we reached my car, leaning against the door, thinking about the alphas that had become my closest friends through training sessions and fights. I'd known Everest the longest, but they were all like family to me now.

The others *would* have my back, I knew that, but I wasn't so sure that I should get them involved. If things backfired now, at least we were the only three who knew anything.

"Only if it comes to it," I finally said.

They both nodded.

"Whatever you say," Everest sighed. "It's not such a bad thing asking for help sometimes..."

I looked at my friend. The lighthearted man that he was, even in a situation like this, remained level-headed and easygoing.

"Maybe. I'll think about it."

Everest beamed.

"Let us know as soon as you hear anything."

I nodded and got in my car, eager to get home but before I could even start my car, my phone rang.

To my disgust, *Harvey's* name lit the screen.

For a second, I saw red as his betrayal came back to me. I didn't want to answer. I wanted to find him and put him in the hospital.

I hit the button.

"How dare you call me, you piece of scum," I spat.

I could practically hear the way he shrank from my angry words.

"Hi Coal," he said after a moment. "How are you?"

He sounded like he was about to piss himself but that made me feel only a bit better.

"How am I?" I asked slowly. "You sold my sister to some gangsters to make a quick buck off my back, Harvey. Me, your own client."

"N-no," he argued. "It wasn't like that."

"Then what was it like?" I demanded.

"Yeah, I-I thought it might work in our favor to set something like this up. Throw the fight and make a quick buck, you know?"

"So you suggested the whole idea?" I asked, a growl rumbling through my chest.

"No, no. I thought they would let me convince you! I didn't know they would take Asha! Please, believe me!"

"Why though, Harvey?" I demanded. "We were making plenty of money winning."

Suddenly it clicked and I threw my head back against the headrest.

"You owe them money," I said.

"Y-yeah," he admitted. "I owe them. I thought this would be a way to pay them back."

I snorted.

"How is that working out for you?"

He was silent.

"Look," he eventually said, his voice coming out a little stronger, "I wanted to call you to make amends before..."

A chill traveled through me.

"Before what, Harvey?"

He was silent.

"Tell me first," he said. "Are you ever going to forgive me? We can go back to a professional working relationship. No more screw-ups, I promise."

I couldn't help but laugh out loud.

"Are you fucking joking?" I suddenly snarled.

Harvey hummed softly.

"I thought you might say that," he said quietly. "I was just thought it would be fair to give you a chance, Coal, considering what a mess I got you into."

"A chance?" I asked.

"Your omega," he said. "The one you stole. Abram isn't very happy about it... Not to mention the Belkin brothers losing all that money and Lambert... you beat the shit out of him, nearly killed him when he was supposed to win."

I stilled, my heart racing.

"What are you talking about?" I asked slowly.

"I'm talking about the fact that I owe these guys. All of them now. And they all want you to pay. And I have to help them get what they want..."

My claws shot out of my nailbeds.

I had to flex my grip on the wheel to keep them steady.

"Harvey," I said slowly, "whatever you're going to do, don't do it."

It was his turn to laugh, a soft, mocking chuckle.

"I gave you your chance," he said. "Now, I'll give Lambert his."

"For *what*?" I demanded. "What the hell does this have to do with him?!"

"That was supposed to be his big break. I guess he wants revenge. I don't know," Harvey said nonchalantly. "And he's willing to pay for it, of course."

"And that's all you care about," I snarled. "Nothing matters to you but money. Not loyalty, not *anything*."

"Maybe you should stop worrying about me," Harvey replied, heat in his voice for the first time since I'd met him, "and start worrying about your skinny little bait wolf!"

He hung up as my blood ran cold.

I'd thought that in my own home, my omega would be safe, that no one would dare challenge me over something so important. I'd been a fool.

Chapter Thirteen

Ember

The longer I waited for Coal, the more I began to *itch*.

It was one thing when he had been here distracting me from my thoughts but being alone in this big house made room for my mind to race.

I explored every room, even peeking into little Asha's room. Her bed was small and still rumpled from when she'd last climbed out of it, so it felt wrong to enter, like I might disrupt the place.

Eventually, I ended up sitting curled up on the

couch, not daring to touch the TV or the fridge, even though I didn't think Coal would mind if I did.

Apparently, being locked in a cell with no autonomy whatsoever did something to a person's confidence. Who would have thought.

I snorted, berating myself silently, but unable to shake the feelings settling over me as I tried unsuccessfully to process what I had been through.

I didn't think I was okay... I didn't think I ever would be again.

And now that I'd been separated from the life I'd lived before being kidnapped, I didn't think I ever had been okay to begin with.

My life had been a train wreck from step one. Aside from my brother, I wondered if anyone had ever loved me or cared for me.

Coal was offering me that now, and I found that I wanted it, but everything else kept hitting me over the head in the meantime.

How was I supposed to get over everything and just move on as though it hadn't happened?

How was I supposed to relish the sunlight with the shadows clearly around me?

I couldn't even bring myself to pick up the remote, for god's sake. Mostly because I didn't know if I was allowed, but I also couldn't face the vapid worlds on the screen. The sitcoms and pretend dramas... Real life was far darker than anything seen on TV.

A soft *click* in the stillness of the house made me jump. And then I held my breath.

That wasn't a normal sound. It was distinctly the sound of the front door lock being touched or tinkered with.

I remained dead still, listening with all my shifter hearing for the sound of a key sliding in. I may have been too weak to shift as recently as I'd tried, but my ears seemed to be getting stronger, even in human form. Perhaps the warm food and comfortable rest was working fast to replenish me.

There was a moment of silence. Then that clicking sound again, quickly followed by a scratching.

It wasn't Coal returning home. Someone was trying to break in.

And I *knew* that it was someone looking for me.

Suddenly, I was moving, my entire body trembling with a burst of adrenaline as I shot to my feet and spun around, looking for somewhere to hide. Then, without thinking, I bolted up the stairs.

Coal's room was soaked in our scents. Maybe

they wouldn't notice me in there. Maybe they would just think our scents lingered there together.

I threw myself into the room, then into the open closet, pulling it shut behind me, trying to remain quiet just as I heard the door swing open downstairs.

My heart was thudding so hard that it drowned out all noise until I heard a voice.

"Come out, come out wherever you are."

A chill traveled over me, quickly followed by an overwhelming sense of understanding.

Of course. The universe didn't want me to have this. Not the house, or the money. Not the family. Not Coal.

I'd never been given anything good in life, so *of course* someone would arrive now to take it all away from me.

I clenched my shaking hands, anger overcoming me, blinding me with rage.

Why? Why? Why is this person here? What do they want from me? Why do they think they can just have me?

"I know you're here, you little slut," the intruder growled as he climbed the stairs. "We were watching the house. We saw the high and mighty Redwood leave here without you."

He laughed and the sound echoed through the corridor toward me.

"How does that make you feel, huh?" he asked. "Your new alpha obviously cares more about his sister than he does about his own mate."

I nearly laughed. The fact that Coal cared so much about his little girl that he was willing to sacrifice our mating time together meant that he was someone special. It meant that he had morals and a heart. It meant that he was the only person I would trust.

"How about you come away with me?" he asked, stopping in front of the bedroom door, his voice chillingly low. "I can give it to you good..."

He stepped inside and the strong scent of his alpha anger swept through the room, seeping through the small gap in the closet door. It was familiar. And I'd scented it recently.

Suddenly, I realized who he was. The other alpha from the fight. *Lambert.* Coal had already won. What the hell did he want with me?

"What do you think?" he asked in a whisper.

There was no need to speak any louder. He was just on the other side of the closet. He knew that I was in here.

"Are you ready to make the Redwood suffer?" he

asked, gently scratching the door with his claws. "I'm here to take what was meant to be *mine*."

Normally, an alpha's anger would make an omega cower, but all I could feel was fury.

He threw the door open but I didn't even see him standing there. All I saw was red.

It was like every person who had ever wronged me had taken form in this alpha. He was the last straw.

I couldn't accept anything bad happening to me ever again. I had hit my limit. It was this life with Coal or dying trying to keep it. There was no in-between.

I leaped at him with all my strength, and only when my teeth latched onto his face did I realize that I had shifted.

I had shifted!

For the first time in months, I was whole. I had never felt more empowered and it was perfect timing.

Lambert fell back with a surprised shout. I landed atop him, feeling bone under my fangs as we jostled, and then I ran my claws over his chest and thighs, trying desperately to cut through his clothes and skin until suddenly, I was flipped off of him.

I crashed into the dresser, sending everything

atop it cascading onto me, including the big-screen TV.

Before I even got my bearings, a large jaw clamped onto my ankle, and I was pulled from the wreckage none too gently.

I tried to scamper out of his hold, but he was too strong. When he released me, I tried to swing around to face him, to bite him again, but his teeth latched onto the back of my neck, biting down hard.

Every time I tried to move, his teeth tightened even more, but that didn't stop me, not until I was flat on my belly, the larger wolf atop me, holding me in such a way that I couldn't move even if I tried.

I lay there, panting, pinned under his impressive weight, and then suddenly, he was human again, his large hands holding my arms down, his face still pressed to the back of my neck.

He started to laugh, the sound deep and reverberating through me in pure ecstatic joy.

"Mm," he moaned, pressing his face behind my ear, "I like an omega who can fight back."

"Oh yeah? What about an alpha?"

Coal's voice growling the question was all the warning either of us got before Lambert was tackled off of my back.

I gasped, struggling to my feet on limbs gone numb from the angle I'd been held down at.

Coal had gotten Lambert off of me, but now they seemed intent on reliving the fight they'd had in the ring only yesterday.

They jumped each other, still in human form. Coal didn't look at me; his attention was focused on Lambert, his expression twisted in fury.

He got a good hook in, knocking Lambert into the bedside table. He stumbled and fell onto the bed.

Coal didn't waste any time, leaping on top of him, but the moment he landed, Lambert threw him off, sending him over the other side of the bed.

Immediately, Lambert shifted, but just as he landed on all fours and fur burst from his skin, Coal, still in human form, landed on top of him, flattening him under his weight. Without arms to stop him, he was powerless to do anything as Coal swiftly head locked him, strangling the other shifter with his biceps.

"Ember is mine," he snarled, tightening his chokehold.

Lambert shifted back. Clearly, he thought that he could fight Coal off, but in human form, his hands, scratching at Coals arms, were just as useless.

Finally, his dark eyes drooped and his arms fell limp. But Coal still did not release him.

"He's *mine!*" he spat.

He was going to kill the other wolf if I didn't stop him. And while the idea of Coal defending me and killing anyone who touched me was an altogether *good* feeling, I didn't want the blood on his hands.

I whined, then did it again louder when he didn't seem to hear me.

Squeezing his eyes shut, Coal finally released him.

He took a deep breath, staring down at Lambert's still form. I knew he couldn't look at me until the anger had dimmed from his eyes.

"I'm sorry," Coal breathed. "I don't know what I was thinking... I guess it hadn't occurred to me that they would try to do it twice. I didn't realize how bitter they all were over things not going their way."

I sank down, a strange feeling of peace flowing over me.

Noting my silence, Coal turned to face me.

He took one look at me where I had laid down and then leaped from Lambert's back, coming to kneel at my side instead.

"Ember," he whispered, brushing those strong

fingers through my fur so softly. How could hands that could cause such harm be so gentle too?

"Are you okay?" he asked.

I wanted to reassure him, to tell him that I was only shaken. Maybe a bit bruised, and yes, maybe I had a couple superficial punctures on the back of my neck too, I wasn't sure, but overall, I was fine.

I didn't think I could shift back though, and Coal seemed to understand that, because he bent, scooping me into his arms and standing.

I nuzzled my nose into his scent gland, breathing him in, gaining strength again.

Now that the adrenaline was fading fast, I was just *so* tired.

Maybe Coal was free for the day now. Maybe he could wrap me up in blankets and cuddle me while I slept.

Ugh. I would do anything for that. To feel safe and protected and to just *rest*.

His lips pressed to my pointed ear, my forehead, and the top of my nose as he carried me. Down the stairs we went, as though Lambert wasn't lying in a heap upstairs.

I didn't even know if he was alive, but I could barely bring myself to care.

Somehow, Coal seemed to understand me and

everything that I needed, because he placed me carefully onto the couch and piled blankets and pillows around me.

"I'll be back in a moment to hold you," he whispered into my ear. "I promise that you're safe now."

There was no hesitation in his voice and the moment I heard his words, I faded to sleep.

Chapter Fourteen

Coal

It was strange to move away from the serenity of Ember, sleeping peacefully on my couch, and go back upstairs. Like ascending from light and love into anger and danger.

Lambert had entered my home. He had not only *touched* my omega, but the image of him pinning Ember would be imprinted in my mind forever.

He deserved to die for what he had done. But Ember had seen enough violence, and on top of that, I had other ideas for the despicable man.

I stepped into the dark stillness of my room, overwhelmed by the other shifter's scent and the distressed pheromones from the three of us still lingering in the air, making it stale.

Lambert hadn't moved from where he'd landed on the bed. He was still slumped face down, but I could tell he was still alive, if barely.

Good. That would make moving him easier.

I stepped up to him, unable to keep the grimace from twisting my lips and I spat on his prone form before bending and unceremoniously grabbing him by the ankles and yanking him off the bed.

He didn't so much as twitch.

I dragged him down the hall. When I reached the stairs, my anger turned to satisfaction as I watched the gratifying sight of his head hitting every step as we descended.

Served him right. And the stairs were carpeted so I didn't feel too badly about potentially waking Ember up.

It wasn't until we reached the bottom step that Lambert's already narrow face pinched even more tightly in a wince.

"Not yet," I muttered, hurrying through the hall. He slid faster on the smooth tiles, but as I pulled open the front door, he moaned and started to sit up.

Before he properly opened his eyes, I bent and hoisted his large form over my shoulders.

He groaned, trying to push me off, but we were already at my car.

"Too late, buddy," I laughed as I threw open the trunk.

I threw him inside just as he started to properly come around.

I didn't think the neighbors were close enough to see into the long driveway, but they were still close enough to hear a wolf howling and screaming. I didn't need any more trouble than I already had, so it would be best not to alert the police of what I was doing. The system here in Lunar City was too corrupt to get involved in anyway.

In the back of the trunk, I saw the hand wraps I used for training.

Without second guessing myself, I moved.

My hand locked around Lambert's wrist before he saw me coming.

I hog tied him easily.

It wasn't until the rope was secured that he *finally* seemed to follow what was happening and his entire body reacted.

He thrashed and a guttural shout tore from his throat.

"Let me go!" he shouted.

I laughed, satisfaction dripping from my voice as he continued to howl.

Then, because he could do nothing but make noise, I bent down, gripping his chin roughly to tilt his face toward mine.

His eyes were bright with fury, but it was no match with how I felt.

"This is what you asked for," I snarled. "When you entered my home and attacked my mate, what did you expect would happen?"

His fangs extended and he snapped at me. Disgusted, I shoved his face away. Then using the other hand wrap, I stuffed his mouth.

"Now listen here," I said. "You be nice and quiet, and I'll let you live. How about that?"

For a moment, his panicked gaze fixed on me, looking unsure.

He nodded minutely.

"Good boy," I said quietly.

I slammed the trunk shut and climbed into the driver's seat, worry over leaving Ember again, making me move fast.

Luckily, the traffic seemed to know I was in a rush, and I pulled up in front of Harvey's office building on the edge of Shadow Alley in no time.

Lambert had been quiet for the ride, just as promised, but that didn't mean I was going to give him a break.

I hoisted him unceremoniously out of the back of my car, ignoring his grunt as I dropped him to the ground.

Then, gripping the loose end of the hand tie, I dragged him over the sidewalk and through the front door.

Business people leapt out of my way like I was on fire, eyes wide and staring. I didn't care. I wouldn't be here long enough for the police to show up.

The elevator to Harvey's floor was a silent ride, broken only by the sounds of Lambert struggling at my feet.

Harvey's receptionist screamed when I walked in. That drew Harvey out of his office.

He took one look at me, and all the color left his pinched, rat-face. Then he ran.

I dropped Lambert, jumping after him, not even bothering to shift, because I was so much bigger than him, and really, he didn't warrant the extent of my ferocity.

As expected, he didn't even make it to the back of the office before I was on top of him. I tackled him to the ground, relishing in the sound of his shout and grunt of pain as I crushed his small body under me.

He was already crying, begging for my forgiveness, but that only made me angrier.

"Please!" he whined. "I didn't have a choice!"

My claws slid out despite myself, cutting into his cheap suit and the flesh inside of it until he was crying out in real pain.

I lowered my lips to his ear.

"If I *ever* see you or your little friend again, you will not be walking, or even crawling away. Get it?"

He nodded frantically, tears spilling out of his beady eyes.

Satisfied, I released him, pushing to my feet.

I didn't look at anyone as I left, not even acknowledging Lambert as I stepped over his body. My mind was already elsewhere.

It seemed to take forever to get home.

An oppressive fear filled me as I drove. I was without Asha and had nearly lost Ember on my first day with him. I was a terrible guardian and mate if it was this easy for people to trample on me.

Then again, until recently, I had thought that I was untouchable. I had trusted my standing in society to be a shield.

That was my own fault.

Pulling into the driveway, the house looked the same as normal.

I walked through the house until I was in the entryway to the living room. Ember was still there, just as I'd left him.

His small wolf form made my heart ache.

There was something about him. Something beyond his life as the fight league's prisoner. He came across as such a lost soul. A wanderer. Like you couldn't keep him if you tried... That was my fear anyway.

We were mated now, but we barely knew each other in the physical sense. I'd spent our first day together running around town trying to fix things. It was unnatural to part from a new mate so quickly after our bonding. My whole body felt out of sorts.

Ember deserved so much better. He deserved security and stability. A place to belong.

Watching him breathe in and out, his form a little slip under the covers, I thought, *I should be that place.*

My thoughts wanted to race again, to call up the detective for answers, but it hadn't been long enough, and Ember needed me.

And I needed him.

So, I pushed the thoughts away as best I could and crawled under the covers to wrap around him.

The tightness in my chest eased and I shut my eyes.

* * *

I woke to a tongue lapping my face, gently cleaning me, and a smile lifted my lips before I even opened my eyes.

Ember was watching me with those smouldering eyes, a sad expression on his furry face.

I reached out, stroking my fingers through his thin, dull fur, and massaging behind his ears until his eyes drifted shut in pleasure.

"I'm sorry I wasn't here," I whispered, and those eyes opened again, fixing on me as though to say it wasn't my fault.

His tongue darted out again, licking my cheek this time and I smiled softly.

"I want to talk," I said gently, my fingers absently continuing their ministrations. "Shift back for me."

Ember twitched, a shiver running through him and dipped his nose down, avoiding my gaze.

I shifted closer, even though we were pressed tightly together, nuzzling my face into his neck.

"Come on, my love," I whispered into his warm fur. "You can do it. Shift for me."

He took a took breath and tried again, and pleasure thrummed through me as his body began to change, lengthening and stretching into his lithe human form.

My arm, now around his waist, pulled him closer as he gasped, his body trembling from the effort.

"You did it," I said, kissing his cheek. "Good boy."

He blushed, rubbing his hands over his face to hide it and then turned his rueful gaze to me.

"Are you alright?" he asked.

"Of course I am," I said, shaking my head in wonder. "My sweet mate, worrying about me, when you should be mad at me."

"Why would I be mad?" he asked.

"Because we should have spent every moment together today," I said. "And you were attacked because of me."

He bit his lip.

"What did he want?" Ember asked uneasily. "Why did he come for me?"

"To teach me a lesson," I said bitterly, and Ember reached up, touching my face with trembling fingers.

I found it odd that he hadn't been nervous to

touch me when we'd made love and it occurred to me that it was *this* intimacy of a quiet, loving moment that he wasn't used to.

"It wasn't your fault," he said, his fingertips brushing gently over my beard.

My eyes fluttered shut.

"I'm supposed to be taking care of you."

"You have other stuff to worry about," Ember argued.

I fixed my gaze on him, making sure that he was really watching me.

"Ember, you deserve to be taken care of and loved and spoiled. Will you let me spoil you?" I asked, and I couldn't resist brushing our lips together.

His face tilted up, automatically seeking more, and I obliged, pressing him into the cushions to kiss him deeply, tasting him briefly before forcing myself to pull back.

I shut my eyes, resting my forehead against Ember's for a moment while I tried to remember why I'd wanted to stop.

"I have to feed you," I finally remembered.

Ember laughed breathlessly.

"Can't that wait?" he asked, chewing his bottom lip, and all of my resolve vanished.

I rolled onto him, taking that plump lip between mine and sucking on it while my hands moved over him, making him gasp.

He was already hard, his body reacting to my presence just the way that mine did to his, and we both moaned as our cocks lined up. I pressed down against him, thrusting gently so that our lengths dragged together.

A ragged gasp left Ember's parted lips and I bent my head down, tasting his sweet mouth, holding his head still so I could kiss him while we moved.

His wet tip spurted precome, drenching us both so that our cocks slipped together wetly until we were both moaning and clinging to each other.

His hands reached for my ass, gripping me tightly, forcing me to move faster and push down harder, crushing our lengths between us, encapsulated by the slick heat of our bodies.

"Fuck me," he groaned.

I hadn't wanted to. I'd wanted to take him out and fucking spoil him rotten. To spend every moment of the rest of the day making him feel special and loved. I'd wanted this to be quick, to leave us wanting more, but how the hell was I supposed to say no when he asked me outright?

"Please, Coal," he whined, spreading his legs around my hips and driving the nail into the coffin.

"Fuck, Ember," I groaned in return, unable to find words, unable to do anything but cant my hips down and rock them until my cock was wet from his slick, the tip seeking out his entrance.

I bore down, slipping inside his tight, welcoming heat and my eyes rolled, balls tightening, pleasure tingling through my spine.

"Oh, fuck," I groaned.

I pulled back, leaving just the tip inside, my cock jumping at the loss, tugging at Ember's hole and making him gasp and arch. The cold air helped immediately but the sight of Ember under me did the opposite.

He lifted onto his elbows, watching me, his long, dark hair a mess, t-shirt askew, lips red from being kissed so hard, cheeks flushed.

I had to shut my eyes against the image.

"You're too beautiful," I moaned. "Going to make me come too soon."

"So, come," he whispered, putting his feet down on my calves to leverage himself up.

I took a shuddering breath as he swallowed my cock back into his hole, clenching around my length as he pressed closer, taking it deeper.

His head fell back and he began to ride me, slowly rocking his hips up and down, until his legs were trembling and he was whining from the pleasure.

I could do nothing but remain still, letting him take me.

I'd never experienced an omega like this before. One who took what they wanted.

Ember obliterated every other sexual encounter that I'd had.

Watching him move, his eyes squeezed shut, simply taking from me, made an almost feral possessiveness rush through me.

Again, I had to shut my eyes, to try to breathe through the overwhelming lust and pleasure and possessiveness that filled me. To remain still for him to take what he needed from me.

And he did with knees bent, canting his hips up and down in a slow, sensual movement, taking me deep and squeezing me hard until I was suddenly gripping the cushions under him, a deep growl resonating through me.

"Yes," Ember hissed, "inside me."

He pressed up, taking me all the way to the hilt and squeezed as hard as he could, his muscles flexing, entire body shaking around me as I came.

It was such an intense orgasm that my body jerked, my cock flexed within him, allowing his clenching muscles to drain me of every last drop. My knot thickened deep inside him, and suddenly, he couldn't hold himself up any longer.

His back fell flat on the couch, but his legs wrapped around me and he reached up, keeping me where I was hovering over him as he started to hump me, desperately, knot and all. Tugging it back and forth within him.

It felt better than it had any right to after coming the way I just had, but there was something feral and free in the way Ember was using my body. The way he clutched my hips tightly enough to leave bruises.

Finally, his whole body shuddered and his cock jerked, come spluttering from the tip and, because of his angle, shooting all the way to his face, some of it splattering over his parted lips as he cried out.

I forced myself to wait until the shudders stopped rolling through his body, but the moment he collapsed boneless under me, I was on him, sucking his wet, come-covered lips into my mouth.

Groaning, I kissed him and licked him, tasting his delicious come, cleaning it off his chin and then sucking a hickey onto his neck because I wanted everyone to know that he belonged to me.

"Mine," I growled, and Ember shivered. His arms went around my shoulders, holding me.

"Yours," he agreed, and warmth filled me.

"I'm going to make you so fucking happy," I promised, and Ember chuckled softly. Such a sweet sound, gentle and real, just like him.

I smiled into his neck, inhaling his scent, my happiness growing as I realized how entwined our scents were.

Now, it would be clear to anyone that we were one.

Chapter Fifteen

Ember

An alpha who cuddled.

It was a thought that would have made me giggle before at the absurdity of it. Yet, here I was, with Coal wrapped around me, kissing me and nuzzling me and *cuddling* me. Keeping me warm with his knot still deep inside me, stretching me so deliciously around him, like a puzzle piece slotted into just the perfect place. We clicked together like that. That was how I felt.

I wasn't used to the warm feeling in the centre of my chest and I really didn't know what to do with it, but I supposed that this was what happened when you found the person you were meant to be with.

"I meant what I said," Coal whispered, his breath tickling my ear. "About spoiling you today."

I smiled, a strange giddiness rising inside me.

"Yeah?" I asked.

"Mmhm."

He pressed a kiss behind my ear, making me shiver.

"What first? Food? Shopping?"

I blinked.

I hadn't really thought of what he meant by spoiling me. He was going to *buy* me things?

I used to judge those omegas who went around town on their alpha's arms like they were only there for show, bags hanging from their hands. I had thought they were fools for allowing themselves to be controlled.

But fuck me, I wanted to go to a fancy restaurant and have Coal feed me dessert off his fork. I wanted him to dress me up how he liked and be proud walking next to me.

This mating had already changed me... Or maybe it was the months I'd spent held captive in a cell.

I was tired of judging and struggling. I wanted to be cared for, and Coal was offering.

"Food?" I said tentatively, and Coal purred in contentment.

"You got it, baby," he whispered, kissing me again, on the neck this time.

God, his lips felt good. So soft. His beard was soft too, a gentle tickle whenever he touched me that gave me goosebumps. And the *nickname*. No one had ever given me one as far as I could remember—nothing nice, anyway.

I bit my lip, squirming a little.

To my disappointment, the movement made his slowly softening knot slip free.

We both let out a soft moan at the loss but Coal took a breath, collecting himself and then lifting himself off of me.

"Come on, sweetheart, let's make the most of the rest of the day."

He offered his hand and I took it, letting him pull me to my feet before reaching down and pulling my loose pants back up.

I was a huge mess, but Coal only chuckled.

"Look at us," he muttered. "We should probably shower before we go anywhere."

He led us upstairs, taking me straight to the door

of the washroom in the hallway before giving me a pained look and pushing me inside without him.

"I'd better let you shower alone or we'll never get out of here," he said regretfully.

The way he bit his lip made me think he wouldn't mind that, and I had half a mind to invite him in with me anyway, even though his come was still currently dripping down my thighs.

He'd barely even pulled out of me and I wanted him back in already.

"Go shower," I said and pulled the door shut.

I leaned my forehead against it and grinned, feeling giddy.

This was actually happening.

Me, *Ember*. The street omega. Had an alpha who adored me and wanted to *spoil* me. It was like I'd walked into an alternate universe.

It had to be too good to be true.

I was still shaking from the sex and the overall whirlwind my life had become. The attack earlier, even that seemed like part of the dream, a set-up for Coal to arrive like a knight in shining armour and just *fix everything*.

I paused just as the water turned on, pouring over me too cold at first and then quickly turning to blissful warmth.

It felt so good being here, being with Coal.

Would he really not mind being the rock for me to lean on? He seemed to be offering that stability and I wanted to take it, but it seemed wrong to let him bear the burden of being the strong one all the time. I needed to remember to stay strong. Life wasn't a bed of roses, even though that was what he was leading me to believe.

I shut my eyes, letting the water massage me for a minute while I stood there, wondering what I could do for him in return.

Then, I reached for the bottles on the rack and spent a few minutes washing myself down and smelling all the different soaps.

I felt downright luxurious as I stepped out of the shower and wrapped an impossibly soft towel around myself. My god, were towels supposed to be this fluffy? The rich really *did* have it all.

There was a soft knock on the door.

"I got some fresh clothes for you," Coal said, not coming straight in. The fact that he was offering me privacy made me blush for some reason.

I glanced in the mirror quickly, seeing my wet hair and flushed face, but most of me was hidden behind the towel, so I cracked the door to find Coal looking incredible in gray slacks and a green sweater that set off the creamy tone of his skin and the warmth in his damp hair.

He smiled at me, and my gaze drifted to his yummy lips before I tore them away, fixating on the folded clothes he was holding out for me.

"Thanks," I muttered, pulling them inside and closing the door between us.

I shook them out, seeing what he'd given me and pulled them on self-consciously, avoiding looking in the mirror until I was dressed.

The loose boxers didn't do much to fill out the pants, but the t-shirt under the thick sweater helped. I didn't look as bony as I expected to, even with the outfit swimming on me.

I bent and folded the pants a couple times before opening the door again.

Coal wasn't there but I heard him downstairs, moving around.

I followed the sounds to the kitchen and leaned against the entryway, watching him as he made sandwiches.

When he caught sight of me, his eyes warmed imperceptibly and he set down the knife he was holding, coming to stand in front of me, taking my hands in his own.

"It doesn't look bad," he said, his gaze sweeping over me. "But I want to get you clothes that fit."

He tugged me forward, pulling me into his embrace.

I let him, wrapping my arms around his waist.

"*Mm.* There is something about seeing you in my sweater that's doing things to me," he admitted.

He pressed his nose to my neck, inhaling and making me shiver.

"You smell more like soap than me now," he said and when he pulled back, he was pouting.

I laughed, pushing him playfully.

"No one is going to miss *this*," I informed him, tugging the sweater to the side to reveal his bite mark. "And I'm sure the hulking alpha at my side will set them straight if they do."

He laughed this time, and I realized it was the first time I'd heard it.

Coal's laugh was as big as he was. Boisterous and contagious and I wanted more of it. The happy version of Coal that I was only now glimpsing.

"Hulking, am I?" he asked, pulling me to the counter and pushing a plate toward me.

"I thought we were going to go get food?" I asked, trying to hide my disappointment. He noticed though, of course.

"We will," he promised and bent to kiss my cheek and then my lips in apology. By the time he pulled back, I forgot what he was apologizing for.

"I wanted to take you somewhere nice, but we missed lunch and the restaurant I like doesn't open again until five. So, I thought we'd eat here, do some shopping, and then head there for dinner?"

I nodded, smiling.

"That's perfect," I reassured and he returned my smile, warmly.

We ate in silence. I devoured the food. It was probably basic, but I hadn't had basic in a long time and good bread, spread, and deli meat were enough for me to moan with each bite.

Coal shook his head, watching me.

"I can't wait until you taste the good stuff," he remarked breathlessly.

I blushed, pleasure unfurling in me. Whatever he saw in me that made me attractive to him, I wasn't going to question it. It was starting to feel how I imagined winning the lottery did.

Chapter Sixteen

Coal

When I said I was going to spoil Ember, I meant it.

After the shit he'd been through, he deserved the world, and I would break my back to give it to him. Even with Asha out there somewhere. Even with my heart in my throat every time I thought about her. Ember shouldn't have to worry the way that I was worrying. He was too special.

There weren't many omegas out there who wouldn't complain after being left alone on their first mating day. There were even fewer who would pick out the cheapest items in the store to try on.

"Stop checking the price tags," I warned as his eyes popped at the price on a pair of pants.

"These are three hundred dollars!" he said. "You can get the same thing for twenty at—"

"They're not the same," I insisted. "These ones are designer. Those ones were made in sweatshops by children."

He grimaced, still looking hesitant.

"But—but what if you need the money to get Asha back?" he asked quietly.

My gaze dropped to the floor, taking in Ember's loose clothing on the way down. He was even in a pair of my shoes. They had to be tied as tightly as possible and he was wearing two pairs of socks to fill them out, but he was still shuffling around in them.

It was sweet of him to worry and he wasn't wrong. I might need all the money I had to get either Asha back or to keep Abram from trying to take Ember back. This wasn't the life that I wanted to give my mate. This wasn't the life I normally lived.

Aside from training with the team and fighting, I took Asha swimming at the local pool, we went to the playgrounds, we snuggled in front of the TV, and so on. On weeknights, I made her lunches for the next day and I walked her to the school bus every morning. I was *domestic*.

I wasn't someone wrapped up in gangsters and fighting out of the ring. Not since I'd joined the fight league anyway.

That was the version of life that I wanted to welcome Ember in to. Not this.

The fact that he hadn't even *met* Asha yet made me ache.

But I pushed that aside once more to try to reassure him.

"You *need* new clothes. Also, I don't think a couple hundred dollars will stop me from paying for her safe return. I'm not counting down to the dollar," I lied, letting my hands run down the length of the loose sweater he wore.

"Really?" he asked, looking up at me hopefully.

I nodded, smiling softly at the relief in his eyes.

Asha was going to love Ember when she met him. Hopefully soon.

It had been hours already. Was Alvy close to finding her yet? I opened my mouth, on the verge of telling Ember about that part of my plan. But he'd already had enough on his plate.

Instead, I stroked back his long, wavy, black hair. There were tangles in it and I made a mental note to pick up other things for him too. A comb, toothbrush, other toiletries. He was starting from scratch in all ways.

And he seemed to understand that, because he stopped arguing. Although he still seemed overwhelmed with the choices until I started picking things out for him.

"What about this?" I asked, holding up a green shirt.

He shrugged, still looking lost and I guessed the biggest part of his issue with this was that he wasn't used to shopping in general, let alone when someone else was buying.

I showed him a few more items before realizing that he was just nodding at *everything* I suggested.

Sighing, I walked through the store, picking things out while he trailed behind me.

Finally, I handed everything to him and pushed him toward the changing rooms.

"I'm sorry, you're only allowed to take in five items at a time," the employee there said. Then she met my gaze and her eyes widened. "Oh! I'm sorry, are you the Redwood?"

I smiled, nodding, and her wide eyes flew to Ember.

"I heard what happened," she said. "It was on the news."

I highly doubted that. Probably the sports highlight, but I wasn't the first fighter to decide that I wasn't leaving without the bait wolf. It certainly wasn't anything sensational.

"We'll just try these on," I said, and she nodded, letting us through.

I steered Ember into one of the rooms, grinning at him as I pulled the curtain shut between us.

"I want to see everything," I informed him, taking a seat on the large ottoman in the middle of the change area.

"Okay," he said, laughing shakily.

I sat patiently, facing the beige curtain that hid him and, for some reason, my heart started to thump in anticipation.

It felt like I was about to get a little show. I got to see my own mate dressing up just for me.

For a while, I sat there, listening to the shuffling as Ember changed.

Eventually though, as the sounds continued, I realized he wasn't planning on opening those curtains.

I stood up, a little bit hurt, despite myself.

When I pulled back the curtain, Ember nearly jumped out of his skin.

He was dressed in a pair of black jeans and the emerald green t-shirt.

"Are you not planning on showing me any of them?" I asked.

At the look on his face, I frowned, realizing he was trying to hide behind the jacket I'd picked for him.

"What's wrong?" I asked.

He bit his lip, looking miserable.

"Nothing fits me," he finally said in a small voice.

I reached out, gently prying the jacket from his grip.

He was indeed swimming in the outfit. Which surprised me, honestly, because I had picked only extra smalls.

I met his embarrassed gaze and slowly reached out, letting my hands reach around his waist. Even through clothes, my fingers nearly met.

More unbearable anger and frustration and sadness took root inside me. I grit my teeth.

"Did they even feed you at all?" I asked quietly.

Ember's lip trembled until he bit down to stop it.

"Sometimes," he finally said.

I had to hold back my feelings. This wasn't the time to go on a killing spree, but Abram was suddenly on the top of my list. The bastard threw lavish parties. Nearly every month he rented out entire clubs for events. After fight nights, he often took fighters on trips or booked out hotels.

The guy was rolling in it. And all off my back, if I was being honest about it. I brought in the crowds.

And that gave me an idea. One that would perhaps fix things where Ember was concerned.

It wouldn't fix things with Asha though.

My stomach squirmed again at the thought that she was still out there somewhere in Lunar City. And here I was, shopping with Ember. I just didn't seem to be able to be at ease, and even the idea of it made guilt hit me like a wave.

I swallowed and pulled him in close. As usual, his lovely soft scent and the mix of our pheromones soothed me.

My eyes drifted shut, face dropping to rest in his hair.

"Are you okay?" he asked, tentatively putting his thin arms around my back.

I nodded, releasing a deep breath.

"I'm okay, love," I whispered. "Let's just take this one step at a time."

Ember nodded resolutely.

"This outfit seems close enough to fitting," he said. "It's the only one that stayed up."

"Let me see the rest, too," I said.

He nodded and looking guilty, gently pushed me out of the room and drew the curtain.

I blinked, my stomach sinking at the fact that he didn't want me in there with him. He obviously wasn't that comfortable with me yet. I didn't know what to do to change that. All I did know was that it added to the ache in my chest.

But I would be patient for him and whenever he was ready to open up for me, I would be here with only love. No judgment. I would support him in every way.

The curtain opened, exposing Ember in a large purple sweatshirt. Something about him in it made me feel like I was on a ride at the fair.

"That one really suits you," I said, smiling gently.

"Really?" he asked. "But it's so big."

"It looks intentional though," I argued. "You look so... cute, I guess."

"Cute?" he repeated incredulously, his cheeked reddening.

He looked down at it, then ruffled his already messy hair.

"Um. What about the pants?"

"They're nice too," I said. "I'll get you a belt for them."

He nodded.

"And the rest?" I asked.

He pulled the curtain shut again, still blushing.

So damn sweet. I just wanted to suck on him like hard candy.

In the end, we left with everything that he could wear that looked good when layered or held up with belts. Two pairs of pants. Three shirts. A sweater and the bomber jacket.

"Shoes next," I said.

Chapter Seventeen

Ember

Coal seemed determined to live up to his promise of spoiling me. He got me shoes for all occasions. Flats, slides, dress shoes, runners. Then right after that, he dragged me to a bath store and bought me everything that my gaze lingered on.

By the time we were done, I felt fuzzy and warm inside with a blush that just wouldn't leave my cheeks.

It still felt strange to be taking from him. It felt wrong. Especially with his child out there, stolen. Not to mention that Abram wanted him to pay for me and earlier today I had been attacked in his—*my* own home.

The whole situation made me feel like at any moment now the rug would be pulled out from under me. *Again.*

I tried to ignore that as we ate dinner.

He was right: the food at this place was orgasmically good.

I'd never had high-end food, but two courses in, I was ready to pledge allegiance to the chef.

I licked the butter sauce off of my fork after swallowing whatever I was eating.

"Oh my god," I moaned. "I had no idea food could taste like this."

"We are coming here every day," Coal informed me, scooping some of the food off of his own plate to add to mine.

I wanted to argue but accidentally scooped more up with my fork and ate it.

"What is this stuff?" I asked through a mouthful.

"Lemon butter scallops," he said, his gaze fixed on my lips.

He licked his own absently, his food forgotten.

Warmth tingled through me.

Maybe it was the fact that Coal kept looking at me like he couldn't believe his luck. Like I was precious and special and maybe even worth every penny that the fight league wanted for me.

I swallowed, my gaze dropping to my plate as the issue of money came back to me. Never having enough of it seemed to be a theme in my life. And he needed it for Asha. No matter how he tried to placate me, I knew that. I'd dealt with enough of the scum of Lunar city to know how it all worked. When gangsters were involved, money was the only thing that would satisfy them. The fact that they'd lost money on Coal's fight was especially reason to believe that they'd want pay back.

"Did," I faltered, trying to remember how to speak, "did you find out anything about Asha's whereabouts?"

Coal's gaze darkened.

"Not yet" was all he said.

He turned his attention back to his food, but I could tell he wasn't tasting it. That was sacrilege, but I couldn't blame him right now. Not when he looked so lost.

"I know the streets," I suddenly said. "Maybe there's something I can do."

Coal gave me a look filled with affection and gratitude at the offer, his lips lifting gently, but he shook his head.

"What could you do?"

I shook my head, thoughts racing.

"I'm good at blending into the shadows," I said eagerly. "I know others who are the same. I could ask around, see if anyone saw her or the people who took her... narrow down their location and wait and watch until I find them... I'm *sure* I could."

Coal's soft smile turned into a frown.

"You could really do that?" he asked.

"Of course. A bit of facing the cold and keeping still—well, I've dealt with worse."

Coal's frown deepened and he reached out. I took his offered hand, warmth spreading through me as he linked our fingers.

"You're an omega," he said thoughtfully. "How you could possibly blend into the shadows before is beyond me. I mean, maybe now that you carry my scent but—"

His voice faltered as he realized the truth. His gaze fixed on mine sharply, searching, and I shrank back, suddenly wishing I could take it all back. My heart seized and I looked down at my nearly empty plate, waiting for him to say something.

It seemed to take forever.

"How many were there before me?" he asked slowly, his voice a deep, dangerous rumble.

I pulled my hand out of his grip, hiding them both in my lap.

"I'm not sure," I forced myself to admit.

On the streets, I often carried the scents of other alphas. Especially any with an oncoming rut and some extra money. Sometimes I even enjoyed the intimacy, feeling briefly needed until their rut passed and I was discarded again. Whenever I went into heat, those were my worst times. Feeling vulnerable with strangers from the streets wasn't my idea of fun. It felt worse afterward knowing I had no control and knowing that the alphas who wanted me in those moments knew that and didn't care.

I swallowed, chanced a glance up and saw the way Coal's jaw was clenched before looking quickly away. A darkness settled over our table; my own emotions mixed with Coal's and the result was a sickening feeling in the pit of my stomach.

Coal took a deep breath, releasing it slowly, but the feeling of his anger only intensified.

Biting my lip, I forced myself to reach across the table and touch his arm, trying to calm him. I wasn't afraid of Coal anymore, even though only a day ago he'd completely lost control. But I didn't want to push him either. After all, his anger had been sparked by the prospect of any alpha coming *near* me, let alone fucking me.

"I've been alone most of my life," I said, still not looking at Coal. "I found a way to blend in early and stay out of trouble."

Coal was silent for a moment, his arm a tense line of thick muscle.

"How old were you?" he asked.

His question finally drew my gaze because he didn't sound angry. His expression was guarded when our eyes met. I couldn't tell what he was thinking but he didn't seem mad.

He placed his hand over mine where it rested as though to comfort me.

"Tell me, Ember," he whispered. "How old were you?"

"When I—"

"On your own, homeless... when did it happen?"

"It was gradual," I said, glad Coal had cut me off. I'd thought he was asking how old I was the first time I'd let an alpha use me and I didn't think he'd like the answer. Now memories floated back to me.

My home, which had been unstable from the start, had fallen apart to nothing. Even the small comforts I'd clung to, like a bed, were lost.

"I was about seven when it started. My mom...

she was on something for a long time, not sure what because she never used in front of me. She'd tell us to 'go play' whenever certain men came around... Then at some point, she just stopped coming home. Foster —my older brother—he got mixed in with some people, became their errand boy or something. I'm not sure exactly. He took care of me as best he could for a twelve-year-old."

Coal cursed, watching me intently, his gaze now filled with nothing but concern.

"Where is he now?" he asked.

I shook my head, a bitter smile touching my face.

"It was like deja vu," I said, the haunting images of my brother returning to me. "At the start we'd hold onto each other all night long to keep warm. He was the only thing I had left. Then he started to go missing, sometimes for days at a time. Eventually, he just didn't come back, just like my mom. I have no clue what happened to him."

My optimistic side hoped he'd been offered a job and been swept away to a different life filled with fun and adventure and comfort and maybe even love. My realistic side offered me images of his pubescent body in a ditch somewhere, long forgotten. In my heart, I knew that Foster never would have left me.

I squeezed my eyes shut, pushing the images down.

"I'm so sorry," Coal whispered, stroking my knuckles.

I swallowed down the lump in my throat, unsure why I'd even started this conversation, except that I didn't want Coal to hate me for the things I'd done. I wanted him to understand.

"You never caught wind of what happened to him?"

I laughed bitterly.

"As soon as he went missing, I started presenting as an omega. Things got dangerous after that. I had to lay low to protect myself."

How could I openly say what happened next? How did I explain that with some guidance from other street omegas, I'd started to take alphas to satisfy my heats and theirs whenever I could?

I looked up at Coal, met his sad eyes and found that all the necessary words left me.

Surely, I'd said enough. Coal could piece the rest together... I didn't need to explain only to make my mate sadder.

"Come on," Coal said. "Let's go home."

The rough tone of his voice coupled with the look in his eyes made me think he wanted to hold me again. I hoped that was the case because I was quickly becoming addicted to being in his arms. And while I had enjoyed being taken around by him, being out and about hindered getting the things I really wanted, like cuddles.

Coal didn't say anything as he paid but he kept looking at me, his gaze dark and sad. I knew he was thinking about everything I had told him, probably imagining what it had been like for me.

I wondered what it would have been like had Coal found me out there. My fated mate appearing on the street to sweep me away. For some reason the thought nearly brought tears to my eyes. It was too much of a fairy tale. Maybe I needed to be at rock bottom to believe this was real.

We stepped outside, into the chill spring air and suddenly Coal's arms came around me, pulling me into a bear hug that I hadn't thought I needed. These were old wounds after all. But the moment I was pressed against that strong chest, pain stabbed straight through my heart like it was fresh.

I took a shuddering breath, sucking in Coal's comforting scent. I should stop poking at that old wound, wondering what had happened to Foster.

Coal pressed our foreheads together, holding my face, stroking my cheeks and then lips with his thumbs. When he tilted and kissed my lips, I felt like I'd been waiting an eternity for it. I pressed in hungrily and the momentary passion of our lips crashing together and tongues tangling soothed and distracted me from the mess my life had been.

I didn't mean to bite down, but my teeth cut into Coal's bottom lip.

He groaned and with a sudden push, flattened me against the side of his car, moaning as he deepened the kiss, pressing down on me with his hips and hardening cock.

I gasped, arching up into him, eager for more when Coal's phone started ringing.

Neither of us stopped right away. Coal kept kissing me, nipping my skin, and I clung to him, my hands drifting to the alpha's muscular ass, squeezing him through his jeans.

Coal sucked my bottom lip, a heated growl rumbling in his throat. He rocked his hips against mine a few more times—but I could feel his thoughts starting to race. I pushed his shoulders gently and, with a heavy sigh, he dropped his head onto my shoulder and reached into his pocket.

An unknown number lit the screen of his phone.

"It might be about Asha," he said.

"Answer it, quick."

Coal did, holding it to his ear.

"Coal Kent speaking."

He fell silent as a woman's perky voice carried to my keen ears.

"Hello, I'm calling from the Lunar City Bank to return your call from this morning."

Coal stilled, seeming to consider what to do.

"Can I call you back in about twenty minutes?" he asked.

"Yes, I'll be here for another hour," she said.

He hung up with a soft groan and bent his head down, breathing me in for a moment.

"I'll still be around when you're done talking to her," I reminded him. "This is important."

Coal looked at me, gaze filled with so much regret that it was almost funny. Almost.

"It *is* important," he agreed. "If I don't find Asha by Sunday night, I'll have to have the money ready on Monday morning."

"Then let's get home so you can talk to her."

Sighing, Coal dragged himself away from me.

I climbed into the car, taking my seat next to him on the comfortable leather.

It was hard not to watch him while he drove. I was trying not to be too disappointed at the interruption. It was ridiculous the way I wanted sex so bad. I had never been like this. Sex had always been easy to come by and satisfying but not mind blowing. But there was just something about the way Coal felt against me. His touches seemed to go deeper than skin. It was almost spiritual.

I swallowed, aware what that meant. Yet again, I was blown away that this had happened to me, especially after our recent conversation, which made my past feel so fresh.

I'd gone from the bottom of the barrel to one of the lucky few who had found his soulmate.

"I'll just be a few minutes," Coal said as we entered the house.

He already had his phone in his hand, but he bolted the door behind me and went through the rooms, making sure that nothing was amiss.

"I don't think we'll have two break-ins in one day, right?" I asked, trailing after him.

After checking behind the last bath curtain, he turned and swept me into another of those all-encompassing hugs. He pressed his nose into my hair.

"Best to be sure," he said and pressed a kiss to the top of my head. "Why don't you go watch TV while I deal with this?"

I nodded, watching as he walked to the office,

sealing the door behind himself without a backward glance.

My stomach squirmed with unease as I realized that Coal only had until tomorrow night to get Asha back on his own, yet he had spent most of the day with me. I was too much of a distraction.

Chapter Eighteen

Ember

Hours later, Coal was still locked away upstairs in his office. I knew; I kept casually walking by the door, unable to help myself.

Despite myself, I was hoping that one of the times I passed, the door would open, and Coal would pull me in to hold and reassure me.

Ugh, what is wrong with me?

I had been so ready to get away, but now a life of solitude in the wilderness didn't seem as appealing as a life with my mate did. It was alarming to me how quickly I was abandoning my desire to escape expectations and just be free. Yet, I wanted this to work out. I wanted to see what life would be like with Coal. Not because he was a fighter, and rich, but because he was everything I thought couldn't be real. It was like he was made for me. All my deeply buried wishes were there in that one man who wanted to give me the world.

He didn't seem to understand though, that I wanted to give him something in return too.

I wanted to give him Asha.

I knew I could find her. I just needed a bit of time.

Coal would never let me, though. He would probably throw a fit if I told him I was going to hide out under bridges and in alleys all night. I understood that too.

That meant I had to be patient and staying out of the way. That was probably the only way he'd actually find her. I was clearly in the way of her search. Coal had been completely preoccupied with me. And I had allowed it.

Frustrated, I went to the bedroom, ready to wash my face and collapse in bed and wait for Coal, but when I caught sight of myself in the mirror, I paused.

I'd barely spared the ones in the bathroom a glance since arriving here and I had been grateful that my small changeroom at the shop hadn't had one, aside from the large one in the waiting area, which I'd pointedly ignored. I hadn't wanted to see how bad the new clothes looked on my frail body. I wanted to pretend I didn't know what I had become.

Now though, I looked into it willingly, allowing what I saw to weigh down on me.

The clothes weren't as bad as I thought they would be. I looked clean this time, unlike when I'd seen myself before the fight. Some of the shine had already started to return to my long black curls, but they still hung limply. My cheeks weren't as gaunt either.

A few more days of regular food would fill me out even more. Still, I didn't look like much of an omega. Aside from a brief period when I'd been young and soft and not as street worn, I never had. I was tall and somewhat masculine. More like a beta. There was nothing for an alpha to lust after here, I decided. Meanwhile Coal was the epitome of an alpha, so large and gruff and fucking *sexy*.

Could he really be so attracted to me?

Insecurity eating at me, I turned away, deciding to take Coal's advice and watch TV for the distraction.

I passed the office, heading to the stairs but at the

last minute, my steps slowed despite myself. I inched closer to the door, listening.

Maybe it was wrong, but he'd been in there for hours, and well... weren't we supposed to be partners now? Why was he hiding away in there? What did he want to keep from me?

I pressed my ear to the thin wood. Coal's voice was easy to make out and I was immediate filled with sympathy at the defeated tone of his voice.

"I know I just bought the house," he was saying. "That doesn't change the fact that I have to sell it."

I frowned, confusion filling me as Coal went on.

"I don't have enough. I just got off the phone with the bank. We were going back and forth. They had me sending them a shit load of paperwork, calculated all of my assets and expenses, I mean right down to my phone bill, Seymour, and it still wasn't enough to get Asha back."

He was silent for a beat.

"If the guy doesn't find her by Monday, I have to hand over the keys and take out a loan for the rest. She needs to be with her dad... That's not even addressing the payment for Ember."

Coal sighed heavily and a long silence followed as he listened presumably to Seymour. I finally pulled away. I edged quietly from the door and found myself sitting in the kitchen, looking out the window at the big empty yard. The conversation explained a few things, really. Coal had just bought this house. That was why the rooms seemed a little bit empty and extra clean and organized. It also explained why he was spending time with me instead of every minute out there looking for her. He had someone else on it.

It seemed like no time passed at all before Coal stomped down the stairs and found me still gazing out the window. He wrapped his arms around me from behind and breathed me in the way he did when he wanted to calm down.

I clung to his strong arms for a moment, aware that Coal was taking comfort from me. He needed it.

"Are you hungry?" he asked.

I shook my head.

"No, I'm okay."

I was impressed with how solid my voice was. I really sounded like nothing was wrong while everything felt like it was already crumbling down around me.

Coal *tsked* and went to the fridge.

"We're trying to fatten you up a bit," he said. "Don't feel shy. You can take anything you want."

"Sorry," I muttered, barely listening. I was too

caught up in watching Coal: the confident way he moved, the narrow line of his hips, his broad shoulders. Coal had some hardships in his past too, but he'd made something of himself. He was rich and famous now in Lunar City. He was *the Redwood*, big and unshakeable. That was what the nickname meant. To see him being brought down like this seemed wrong.

Worst of all, I felt a gut-deep need to protect my alpha. I wanted to see him smiling and happy, yet my very presence was adding to the issue. Coal was sacrificing a lot to be with me: his home, his sister, potentially his job...

If he paid the price for me, would he have enough to get his sister back?

If I was gone, could he keep the home he'd worked so hard for?

We had both had it rough growing up. Was it really worth going back to having nothing?

A small part of me, deep in the back of my mind, whispered, *If we have each other, we won't need anything else.* But I knew that wasn't true. I used to think silly things like that as a child and reality had given me a cold, hard slap.

I looked at Coal, the strong lines of his broad

back, still disturbed that anyone could take something away from him. It felt like no one was safe.

When Coal looked at me, worry was etched in the lines of his brow. Despite that, he still gave me a smile, a small dimple visible when he shot it my way.

I clenched my fists to stop myself from going to him. Coal had wanted privacy for that call. Clearly, he didn't want my involvement in his issues.

"What do you want to have?" Coal asked. "We're pretty well stocked."

"Anything," I said, although I wasn't even hungry. I wasn't used to so much food and I still felt full from our decadent dinner.

Suddenly, I felt awkward and on display under the bright lights. Coal was fit, healthy, and rich. By comparison, I knew I looked exactly like what I was—a cheap, half-starved street omega who was completely out of place here. New clothes weren't going to change that.

Coal though, to his credit, did not look at me that way. No, when his gaze met mine—which it did frequently as he searched through his fridge, darting to me every couple of seconds—was full of interest and warmth.

Coal wanted to take care of me. It wasn't a bad thing. I didn't know how to say that my stomach could wait. I knew I was too gaunt to be properly attractive, no matter what my alpha said. Coal though was just *so* perfect.

I tried to push down my arousal as I watched him move around the kitchen, unable to look away, but I couldn't. It had been so long since someone had touched me the way he did and *Coal. Ugh.* He smelled so fucking good it was hard to think straight. And the way he fucked me just right—

My grip tightened on the edge of the counter, my cock rock hard, moisture already making me slick down there.

Was I really like this? And here I'd thought Coal was the cliche when *I* was the one sitting here wishing the guy would just come over here and fuck me again.

I bit my lip, squeezed my eyes shut.

A soft moan had them flying open again.

My heavy gaze landed on Coal again. He was still standing facing the open cupboard, his head bowed, broad back to me.

"Are you sure you're hungry for food?" he asked, voice a low rumble that cut straight to my groin. "Or is there something else you want more?"

I swallowed. I wasn't going to play around. I knew very well that Coal could smell my arousal, and I was disgusted with myself for being a stereotype, but not enough to *not* want Coal on me. *Now.*

Slowly, Coal turned, facing me. His pants were stretched over the hard length of his cock, pulling the fabric tight. My face went hot, my mouth dry.

"Well?" Coal asked.

I blinked at him, dazed.

Coal's pheromones were strong. He was so turned on that the air was thick with it, and it was making me dizzy and my hole impossibly wet. I clenched around nothing, trying to ground myself, but even that felt good.

When I forgot to answer, Coal reached down, pushing his pants past his hips, unceremoniously exposing himself. His long, thick cock smacked against his taught abdomen, smearing a slick line from the tip.

"Do you want it?" Coal asked.

I nearly laughed.

"Of course I want it. Can't you tell?"

With that admission, Coal kicked out of his pants and swept forward, coming straight to where I still sat. He pressed between my legs, taking me in his arms, pressing his hard cock into mine. We both gasped and then he was pushing his large hands into my hair, tilting my head and capturing my mouth in a searing kiss.

Coal's lips were warm and gentler than I'd ever expected an alpha's to be. His hands too, so big and capable of so much harm, touched my body firmly and desperately, but never too tight or too hard, like Coal was ever conscious of my frailty.

And with that thought, I was conscious of it again, just as Coal slid his hand under the hem of my shirt. This morning, in bed under the covers, I hadn't thought of anything but how good it felt. On the couch later, he hadn't explored me the way he was trying to now. Under the bright kitchen light, it was different.

Panicked, I held the fabric down when Coal tried to pull it up, not yet catching on to what was happening. The second time I yanked it back down again, he pulled away, breaking our kiss.

"What's wrong?" he asked. His eyes were darkened with arousal, all for me, and I wanted this man to take all of me so badly that it wasn't fair.

"I don't want you to see me."

I'd seen myself in the mirror enough by now that the gaunt image was burned into my retinas. I couldn't bear someone as attractive as Coal seeing the way my ribs jutted from dull, cracked skin.

Coal's gaze darkened further, but this time, not in lust.

For a moment, everything was still. I was sure that Coal was going to argue or force the clothes off of me, but to my surprise, he nodded.

"Let's go to the bedroom," he said, stroking my arms. "We can keep the lights off."

"Are you sure?" I asked, more surprised than anything.

He nodded and pressed a kiss to the corner of my lips.

"I want you to be comfortable."

I followed Coal up the sweeping staircase, down the long hall and through the bedroom door. We didn't speak, and even though Coal's hands never left me—touching my arms, my back, the nape of my neck—I worried that I had ruined the moment. I was still so turned on though. My cock practically ached, my body clenching, wishing to be filled.

I'd fucked alphas all the time before, but aside from my heat, it was always for money, never for my own pleasure. Sometimes, I could barely even get wet for them. But when Coal closed the door behind us, sealing us in darkness, and immediately engulfed me in his arms, I nearly wept with relief.

Coal was still hard for me. I could barely wait to have him inside of me again.

I wanted it so bad. I needed it. It was more than that too. Coal was my mate. Even if I was starting to think being together was a mistake. That I shouldn't stay with him. Why the hell shouldn't I answer my baser needs while I was here? Why shouldn't I get some modicum of pleasure inserted into my otherwise unpleasant life?

I clung to Coal, rutting against him, desperate for some relief as we clutched each other, kissing and touching.

With a groan, Coal turned me, so my back was toward him. I arched back, pressing his meaty cock between my cheeks and gasping at the spark of pleasure there.

Coal groaned, then reached down, shoving my pants off my hips. They fell to the floor, exposing me to the cool air as he pressed his cock tightly to my crease again, this time with nothing between us. He started rocking against me until I was gasping with each rub of slippery sensation, desperate for more but unable to stop meeting his movements with my own.

"You're so wet," he moaned and then, still inserted cozily where he was, he steered me toward the bed. Instead of climbing onto it though, he pushed me gently forward, going so far as to steer my hands into a comfortable position on the soft duvet as though I was some precious, breakable thing.

"You don't have to be so careful," I laughed breathlessly. "It's not like I've never been fucked before today."

I regretted it the moment the words left my mouth. Coal's entire body seemed to harden—and not in the good way.

Fury.

I could feel it pushing off him in waves, his delicious, inviting scent turning hard and bitter.

He bent his head down slowly, lips brushing my ear.

"Don't talk about getting fucked by others. Don't *think* about getting fucked by others. Not while you're here with me. *Please.*"

His grip was harder, but not hard enough to hurt. His voice was strained with the effort of holding in his anger and *sadness*, I realized.

I nodded, guilt filling me.

God, what was wrong with me? Talking about getting it from other alphas to the one who wanted me for good. It was downright mean, and Coal didn't deserve it. He was gentler and more caring than I had thought a fight wolf could ever be. He was better than any alpha I had ever allowed myself to dream about.

"I'm sorry," I whispered, and Coal seemed to melt a little, a sigh leaving his lips.

"We'll talk about it later," he said. He touched my chin, tilting my face to give me a deep, sweet kiss that quickly turned filthy. He sucked my tongue into his mouth, bit my lips and then started kissing down my jaw, the back of my neck. When he got to the scent gland there, he paused, nuzzling it and moaning.

"So good," he groaned. "You smell so fucking good."

My fingernails dug into the fabric beneath me. I returned the sentiment. Coal smelled divine, like the way the sun felt on a warm day at the beach. It went through my skin and lifted me up from the inside. It was better than any high I had ever experienced.

I arched back, desperate for more, and Coal pushed my loose shirt up. This time I managed to push the worried thoughts away and allow my alpha to undress me. The room was dark enough that it didn't matter, but when Coal pulled back, removing his own shirt, I felt a stirring of regret.

By insisting on the darkness, I was missing out on seeing Coal in all his glory.

I could still feel him though, the brush of hair on his chest when he settled back over me, his soft skin and long, thick shaft, wet from our combined desire.

I fell into the sensations, less person than pleasure as Coal worked his way down my body, finding sensitive spots with his fingers and his lips.

When he reached my ass, he bit and massaged the cheeks before licking a stripe down the center, moaning at the way it clenched against his tongue.

I groaned, the ring of my muscles contracting as Coal slid his tongue inside. I wanted to be filled so badly that I could barely stand it.

"Please," I begged. "Fuck me."

Coal let out a shuddering breath and kissed my entrance once more before pushing to his feet behind me and positioning his large cock.

He pressed in smoothly, going deep in one long thrust that made me cry out. When he started to move, it wasn't as clumsy as this morning; it was more measured, more purposeful. It was deep and slow and almost unbearable.

I didn't last long, stretched to the limit with Coal inside me, his cock massaging my prostate with every long stroke. I came with a curse, clutching the covers.

Unable to hold myself up, I pressed my face into the blanket and simply held on as every drop was milked out of me, my cock flexing tightly until I was done.

Behind me, Coal grunted but kept going, fucking me through it until the pleasing feeling of Coal within me turned into arousal again and I was a mess, moaning in pleasure, desperate for another orgasm.

My fingers dug into the covers again, and I held on for dear life as I was given a second mind-melting orgasm, just as good as the last. My whole body was shaking. I felt like a boneless mess, unable to think of anything but the feeling of Coal still pounding into me.

Finally, he bent, burying his face into my neck, his thrusts turning erratic and quick. He slammed his long cock into me one more time, as deep as he could, emptying his cock with a guttural moan, his whole body shuddering.

He collapsed over me for a moment, but quickly lifted onto his elbows over me, gasping for air. Then, he helped me properly onto the bed, pulling my back against his chest and holding me there while his knot grew within me.

I held onto Coal's arms tightly as though afraid that he would drift away.

That was when I *finally* realized that was exactly what I was going to do.

Taking a little dose of pleasure from the man that I now wanted to spend my life with was probably my only compensation.

I had almost always been alone. I was used to it.

Coal though... he couldn't live without his child. He'd already said as much. I didn't blame him. She was practically his daughter after all.

Coal should use his money to get her back.

I wouldn't allow myself to get in the way.

And in the meantime, if I could use my skills to find Asha first, then I would.

Chapter Nineteen

Coal

Lying with Ember was like a little slice of heaven inserted into the chaos that was currently my life. I loved the soft sound of his breathing, the warmth of our skin pressed together.

But as I remained there, my knot still buried deep inside my mate, the unpleasant part of our love-making came back to me.

Perhaps we had skirted around the discussion too many times, thinking it could be left unsaid. I didn't want to think of my omega sleeping with others, but he obviously had. Did he have a choice in the matter?

Did people force him or hurt him? Those thoughts, the not knowing, were turning out to be more painful than hearing all the details ever could be.

I cleared my throat, searching for the words, wondering how to even broach the subject.

A soft snore drifted from Ember, and I sighed, smiling. It would have to wait until later. I didn't have the heart to wake my mate.

Poor Ember had been through so much. It sounded like he'd never had a moment of stability and safety in his entire life.

The thought of him so young, on the streets with a brother who was also a child. They should have had someone watching out for them. He'd never had an alpha, had he? Not even a father figure or alpha brother who was willing to do anything to keep him safe.

At least I'd had that for a time. Before my mother's passing and my father's subsequent downward spiral, my father had been strong and caring. He'd seemed unshakable. A wall to stand with or hide behind depending on the situation. Although I hadn't needed him as much as I had grown. My physiology had a part to play in that. Being an alpha meant I hungered to be the one caring for others, protecting them and keeping them safe.

Now that Ember was part of my family, he would learn; he never had to be alone again.

My knot finally loosened as it reduced, but I didn't move for a few more minutes, keeping my cock warm and soft inside him. It was so comfortable, like being wrapped in a blanket.

Somehow, I fell asleep like that and woke up with early morning light filtering through the curtain, my cock at attention, still buried inside him.

I let out a low moan and gently pulled out.

Ember moaned softly but didn't wake up, and I reached down, gripping my shaft. The skin was a bit tender from spending so many hours inside Ember, but it was worth it for the fulfillment and satisfaction that I felt at that.

I could have spent the rest of time in this bed, parting only for more lovemaking sessions, but Ember needed breakfast. Especially since he was obviously self-conscious of his light frame. I still thought he was beautiful, but I wanted him to be healthy and confident in his own skin.

My own stomach was rumbling. Stress muted my appetite for the last few days and now my stomach had evidently had enough of that.

I pressed a quick kiss to Ember's forehead and carefully extracted myself from his warm embrace.

I pulled my PJs on, and my gaze settled on his slight form under the covers. All the love in the universe bundled up in my bed.

I couldn't wait to get to know Ember better, his habits and tics, his likes and dislikes. I wanted to know him better than I knew myself.

It was so true what people said. Once a bond was made, one mate couldn't be without the other. It was huge, this feeling that I really couldn't live without him.

In the hallway, I paused, hand on the knob, my world sinking again as reality reared its ugly head.

I had to deal with Abram. If Monday came and I didn't have the cash—if they somehow took Ember back into the fight league's underbelly... *Could* they do that? Was I at risk of losing him?

Sighing, I pressed my forehead to the closed door. I had to fix this now, before I got wrapped up in being with my mate again. Before Alvy contacted me with Asha's whereabouts and my plan of action to deal with Lambert and Harvey and the gangsters came into play.

I couldn't allow myself to be so distracted that I lost my mate before we really got to become a family.

I pulled out my phone, hit Abram's name, still unsure what to say. If I gave him the money for

Ember but I didn't find Asha on time and had to pay for her too, what would I do? I would be screwed. I was already short on funds by a long shot.

The line clicked. It took Abram's rough voice answering, the reminder of our usual relationship, and I suddenly knew what I had to do.

"Set up a fight," I found myself saying.

"What?"

"Do the promotions, pick anyone you want."

"Do you not recall that you're on my shit list at the moment?" he demanded. "You ran off with my property."

I had to grit my teeth at Ember being addressed anyone's belonging. How the fuck had I been okay with this before? How had I always turned the other cheek?

"I don't want a payout."

"What?"

"I'll do a fight and you keep everything. That covers Ember, right?"

Alvy hesitated.

"Anyone I want?" he asked.

"Yes. Make it a big show. Draw out the crowds. They'll come to see me."

He laughed darkly.

"Especially after your last fight. You sure know how to make a show."

"So, it's a deal?" I asked.

He huffed, clearly thinking it over.

"You're still in my shit book," he informed me.

I remained silent and finally, he let out a heavy sigh.

"I'm going to send a contract over to your agent," he said.

"No, send it straight to me. I've cut Harvey out."

"Brutal," he muttered, but his obvious lack of knowledge over what had happened gave me a modicum of peace. At least not everyone had been involved in Asha's kidnapping. Not everyone had been trying to make a quick buck off of fucking me over. Then again, he was still doing that now in his own way, with Ember.

I bit my lip to hold in any comments that might make him change his mind and hung up.

Downstairs, I settled on making eggs and toast. We could probably both do with some carbs and protein. Normally I made pancakes because Asha requested them at least once a week. I smiled at the thought, but my heart twisted in pain.

I should be out there, searching for her myself... but in a city like this one, with its dense streets, multitude of back alleys, skyscrapers, Asha could be anywhere.

The detective had said he knew where to start looking. If I didn't hear from him by this afternoon, I would be taking matters into my own hands.

I had until Monday. That meant I had the rest of today to get her back the way *I* wanted to. Otherwise, I would show up with the deeds to the house and everything in my bank account to get her back.

I'd started from scratch before. As a family, we could do it again if we needed to.

Sighing, I turned my attention back to the meal I was preparing just as my phone started ringing.

My heart sped up, sure for a moment that it was the detective calling with Asha's whereabouts. It was an unknown number, though, and a video call.

The moment I answered it, tears stung my eyes at the sight of my little girl.

"Asha," I choked.

"Hi Daddy Coal," she said, big, sad eyes fixed on me.

"What's wrong, baby? What happened? Did someone hurt you?"

My claws were out, digging into my palms, drawing blood. Depending on the next words out of her mouth...

"No. I just want to come home. I miss you," she said and then started sniffling, tears filling her eyes as she looked at me, her childish gaze accusatory. "Why can't I come home yet?"

I bit my lip, trying to calm myself.

"I want you home too. I miss you so much."

My traitorous voice broke. Whoever was with her would hear how much I cared, but for her sake, I didn't mind. It didn't matter if they knew how much he wanted her home again.

"Wool said you don't want me to come home yet."

"Wool?" I demanded. "Is that who you're with?"

Before she could answer, the phone was pulled from her hands and Kai's face appeared, smarmy grin and all. It was like he took the position of younger brother to heart, attempting to be the more unsettling of the two gang leaders. I couldn't believe it, but I actually *preferred* dealing with Alek.

"Listen up, you bastard—"

"I don't think you're in a position to talk to me in that tone," Kai said, smiling. He tilted the camera, showing the way he stroked the silky waves of Asha's caramel hair while he spoke. She looked up but didn't seem to notice the claws he allowed to extend, so near her delicate flesh.

I went very still.

"We're just calling to check in," he said, voice pleasant as he turned the camera back to his smiling face. "We wanted to remind you that Asha wants to come home."

"I thought I had until tomorrow to get the money," I said. My voice sounded hallow and distant to my own ears.

"You do," Kai agreed. "But only until then. She's very eager to be with her big brother again. Isn't that right, dear?"

"Yeah! I want to come home Daddy!"

If they got their way, she wouldn't have a home to come back to.

I swallowed.

"Where do I meet you?"

Kai smiled benignly.

"Crow's Diner. Be there at seven tomorrow morning."

I could still hear Asha's little voice, trying to get my attention just as Kai hung up.

I was left staring at the blank screen, feeling like the world was caving in around me.

Next to me, I had a nice, normal breakfast cooking. Meanwhile, she was being kept by monsters and I had no control over the situation whatsoever.

Suddenly, arms came around me, strong and sturdy, and I leaned into the embrace the moment it was offered to me, taking the comfort Ember had to offer.

"I didn't hear you come down here," I said.

Ember stroked my arm, used the other to take the pan off the stove and then came right back, holding me tightly.

"Are you okay?" he asked, voice small.

I glanced at him, saw the distressed look in his eyes, and managed a nod. It felt weird to lie to my mate, like the world tipped sideways, but I ignored it. I didn't want Ember to have to worry about all of this.

"I guess you heard all that?"

"Some of it... Most of it, actually."

I didn't know what to say.

"Let's eat," I eventually said, gesturing to the food.

Ember gave me a look that I couldn't read but didn't argue.

A strange silence fell over us as I served the eggs. They were burned at the bottom, but I couldn't bring myself to care. It wasn't until we were sitting at the table eating in continued silence that I realized I'd forgotten about the toast. I hadn't even remembered that I should try to engage in a conversation. I was supposed to be making Ember happy, after all, but when I looked at him, Ember just appeared sad and distant, like he was miles away. Thank god he wasn't *actually* miles away. That would kill me. Just as much as losing Asha.

The thought was so upsetting that I set down my fork and took a shuddering breath to calm myself. When I reached for Ember's hand, he took it at once, clinging to me like a lifeline.

"Do you like the food?" I asked.

Ember blinked.

"*That's* what you want to talk about?" he demanded. "Coal, your sister—"

"She'll be with us by tomorrow. I have to trust that she's okay and be patient."

"So, you have the money for her?"

I couldn't meet his gaze but managed a nod, and again, guilt immediately hit me. I could trust Ember, of course, but I didn't want to burden him. Not when he'd only just escaped such a hard life.

"How's the food?" I repeated.

For a moment, Ember looked incredulous, but then, his gaze dropped and fixed on the burned eggs. He picked up his fork again and took a bite.

"Delicious," he said sincerely, and I believed

him. He still looked upset, but his emotions, even through his scent and our bond, were hard to read. He ate every last bite though and eventually he changed the subject.

Ember asked all about me, about my friends, my favorite things to do when I had time.

I found myself telling stories of my fight training, sparring with friends who I met through the club: Seymour, Everest, Aspen, and Aurora. I told him about the park nearby that me and Asha often went to, about the struggle of house hunting in a city overloaded with the wealthy. I told Ember about how strange it was to go from bottom of the barrel to being the guest of honor at parties with riches unlike any I had ever seen. The strange, incomprehensible culture of the elite, who kept their omegas hidden from view until it was time for *Omega Season.*

Ember was enthralled, his eyes wide, asking question after question about me, my life, my experiences. He laughed more than I expected and touched me often, a hand on my arm, shoulders bumping when we made our way to the couch.

We put on the TV and Ember leaned against me, snuggling up tight, like he was trying to get the most of me that he could. Like I was going somewhere.

The realization hit me sometime after the first episode of the baking show we were watching ended.

Ember was acting like this relationship was going to be very short lived. Maybe he thought something was going to happen to me when I went to get Asha back.

I wanted to reassure him but didn't know how to without bringing up the depressing situation once more. If I was lucky, I'd know where Asha was long before morning... and I would barge in on those gangsters to take my sister—and my revenge.

Instead of ruining our lovely morning together with plans and plots that would only worry Ember more, I bent and kissed him on the top of his head.

Ember gripped my shirt tighter.

Neither of us moved from our comfortable position holding onto each other.

Warm and momentarily content in his arms, I couldn't help drifting to sleep.

When I woke up, it was because I was cold and, notably, alone. The TV was still on, now playing the news, something about the mayor's intention to clean up the valley. I would believe it when I saw it.

I sat up, listening for my mate.

"Ember?"

Even without waiting, I knew; Ember was gone.

The very air felt different. Empty. My chest felt like my heart had been carved out of it. I didn't need to search the house to know.

I did anyway, hoping that I would find Ember curled up in our bed. He wasn't, of course. All I found was one of my notebooks, laid open on the kitchen counter, a note scrawled in messy writing.

I won't let you lose your home or your daughter just to have me. Thank you for everything.

A strange, chilling sensation went through my body, like I had been dunked in ice cold water.

Ember thought that I would lose my home if we were together. He thought Asha was more important. True, I would do anything to be with my little girl, but I would do the same for Ember. I loved him.

The deeds to the house... that was my *last* resort. I shouldn't have kept anything from my mate. I should have told him about the P.I.

"Fuck!" I shouted into the silence.

It wasn't too late.

Ember might have just left. For all I knew, he could still be walking down the driveway.

Without thinking, I went after him.

I burst through the front door, saw no sign of my mate, but caught a whiff of his scent, already fading.

Without thinking, I started to shift but promptly stopped as my phone vibrated in my pocket.

I pulled it out, still following Ember's scent, pausing to decipher which direction he'd gone. I would have an easier time following the scent in my wolf form.

"What?" I demanded into the phone, without looking at the number.

"I found her."

My steps faltered at the sound of the P.I.'s voice.

"Where is she?"

"She's being kept in an apartment in Steam Harbor."

"Is she okay?"

"She seems to be. She's fast asleep. I'm looking at her right now."

My heart was racing, imagining her fast asleep in some random bed in Steam Harbor. God, it was so close. Less than ten minutes in my car and I could be there with her.

"Send me the address."

"I'll text it to you now."

Alvy hung up.

For a moment, I stood there numbly before my phone went off with Asha's location.

I looked at it, then lifted my face, inhaling

Ember's quickly fading scent. I wasn't sure exactly how long ago he'd left. Long enough that I couldn't be sure I would find him right away.

It felt like I was being torn in two, but in the end, only one thing made sense.

I *knew* where Asha was right now. I couldn't leave her with her captors for a moment longer.

Lifting my phone, I wrote into the group chat I shared with my closest friends. I'd called each of them while locked away in my office yesterday, to make sure they were on board. They were all at the ready, waiting for me.

Buzzing with adrenaline, I typed and sent a quick message.

I have Asha's location. It's go time.

Chapter Twenty

Coal

I stood in the shadows as the sun set over the harbor, staring up at the building that overlooked it.

It was tall, nondescript, just like all the other apartments in the area.

Asha was on the first floor. I could see the window that Alvy had been watching her from. It was dark, and, from the angle I was at, I couldn't see inside.

Everest and Seymour were on one side of me, Aspen and Aurora on the other.

My heart warmed at the fact that my friends had

answered my call without a question. And Seymour and Aurora both had mates waiting for them at home, yet they'd still come.

The five of us, all big, intimidating alpha fighters at the top of the fight league, were a formidable sight. I hoped anyway.

We were willing to use as much intimidation and force as necessary.

"Someone's coming," Aspen said, voice low.

Finally.

Without a word, the five of us walked to the front confidently just as a woman reached the glass doors. She tapped the fob and opened it without looking up, then stumbled when I grabbed the door, keeping her from shutting it.

She was a beta, slight in form, and, despite the sign that read *Do not hold door open for strangers. SECURITY cameras in effect*, she only glanced at the five of us before deciding not to get involved and hurrying toward the elevator.

Room one hundred and seven was only a minute's walk in the stuffy hallway. A light flickered at the end of the hall, but there was nothing sinister about the place. It was just a fairly new building in an upper middle-class neighborhood. The perfect place to hide a kidnapping.

My skin itched as we came to a stop in front of the door. I didn't know what we would find inside. A pack of alphas guarding Asha? Maybe just Kai himself?

I hoped for the latter.

Without Ember by my side, knowing that he was out there somewhere... it took something from me. A forgiving, loving part of my heart was now hollow and all I wanted was to tear the fuckers in there apart to unleash all the pent-up frustrations that had built over this whole ordeal.

Everest tried the handle quietly. Of course, it was locked. That didn't matter.

I stepped back, braced myself, and tackled the door.

It broke off the hinges, falling into the room with a loud, heavy thud.

Well, that would wake the building.

Without waiting, I shifted, leaping into the dark apartment just as someone jumped up from the couch inside with a shriek.

They had clearly been sleeping there.

I leaped toward them, ready to kill if I had to. My paws landed on the person's shoulders, claws ripping through flesh as they fell back again, screaming.

That was when I realized. It was an omega.

Shit.

I shifted back, still pinning the omega flat against the cushions. She stared up at me with wide, scared eyes filled with tears.

"Who are you?" I snarled.

"S-Sandy," she stuttered. "I didn't do anything. I swear, I just take care of Asha—"

"Where is she?"

"Sleeping."

She pointed with a shaking hand toward the hall. I could see three doors.

I left the omega, following the others as they lead the way.

One of the doors was open exposing an empty washroom. Two bedrooms and an omega sleeping on the couch. That meant there was someone else here.

When the guys threw open the door, it wasn't Asha's room. Another alpha—*Kai*—was already waiting for us. He held a gun up and fired the moment the door swung open.

Seymour fell back with a shout, stumbling out of sight.

"Seymour!" Everest shouted, moving to catch him, but there was no time to see how bad it was because the gun was still aimed at the rest of us.

As one, we shifted.

Somehow, I was gratifyingly the first to reach Kai. I caught the gangster's arm in my jaw and bit down as hard as I could until a satisfying *crack* echoed through the air along with his desperate shout.

The gun dropped from his hand, and he fell to his knees.

Shifting hurt like a bitch with broken bones, so I knew he wouldn't dare. He was too much of a coward.

With every ounce of control I had, I released him and shifted into my human form.

Aspen and Aurora remained as their wolves, one on each side of Kai, ready to take him down with one wrong movement.

Kai didn't try though, only clung to his broken arm, his eyes wild.

I bent and picked up the discarded gun. His face paled.

"Please, don't," he said, voice strained from the pain.

"Not such a confident fucker now, are you?" I demanded.

He was still on his knees, cradling his arm, careful not to touch the spot that turned at the wrong angle. Tears and sweat dampened his skin.

It would be *so* easy to end him now, but I wouldn't use a gun; I wasn't that cowardly. I'd rip him apart with my own teeth.

"You can take your sister and we'll let all this go. No need to get on my brother's bad side. Alek isn't a forgiving man."

I took a shuddering breath, reminding myself that killing Kai would only put an even bigger mark on me.

Instead, I glanced back at Everest.

My friend was crouched on the floor, looking pale. Beneath him, Seymour lay in a pool of blood.

"He okay?" I asked, tense.

"I'll survive," Seymour grumbled, but it didn't look like he could get back up. Where had he been hit?

"Want me to put a bullet in him to make it even?" I asked.

Seymour grinned.

"If he doesn't behave."

Returning his grin, I turned to Kai and reached into his shirt where the edge of his phone was visible. I laughed outright at the way the other alpha jerked back from me in obvious fear.

"Relax, I'm just going to give your brother a ring."

I found Alek's number easily and made a video call, then turned the screen to face Kai where he crouched on the floor in fear.

The second Alek answered the line, he started swearing, shouting, asking who the hell was responsible, threatening anyone who would hurt his brother.

I chuckled and flipped the screen to face me.

"You fucking bastard! You're done!" Alek shouted.

I shook my head calmly.

"You fucked with my family first. You targeted me for no reason. You stole my daughter... This is retribution."

Alek forcefully calmed himself, combing fingers through his unkempt, jet-black hair and shutting his eyes for a moment before he looked at me again, face an expressionless mask.

"What are you going to do?" he asked placidly.

"I'm going to take Asha and leave," I said.

Alek didn't seem to believe me. His gaze darkened, jaw clamping.

"What are you going to do to my brother?"

I considered.

"He shot my friend when we walked in here. I broke his arm in return. Let's call it even."

There was a very long silence.

"Seriously?"

"It was Kai's offer. Isn't that right, Kai?"

I nudged him with my shoe, and he immediately nodded.

"I told them if they leave me alive, they can go. We won't bother them again, right Alek?"

Alek's jaw set even tighter.

"*You* involved me for no reason," I reminded him.

Finally, grudgingly, Alek nodded.

"*Deal.*"

"Don't ever involve me or my fighters in any of your business again."

The gangster nodded.

"You have my word."

Finally satisfied, I nodded and hung up.

I tossed the phone onto the bed.

"We should leave before the whole mob shows up to check on this guy. I doubt they'll keep their word if we're still here."

Kai shook his head.

"We may be a lot of things, but we have honor," he said. "We never break a deal. That's why we take it so personally when someone else does."

He gave me an accusatory look, and I nearly lost

it. I took a step toward Kai, but Everest's hand on my shoulder stopped me.

"Let's not throw that deal out the window by killing the bastard," he said. Then, his gaze filled with worry, he added, "Go get Asha, quick. Seymour needs to get to the hospital. Now."

I managed to hold myself back.

"Come on," I said to the others, backing out of the room.

I sealed it shut behind me, Kai's gun still in my hand.

Aurora shifted back first, going ahead, keeping watch on the front room while I went to Asha's room. Behind me, Everest went back to Seymour's side. The amount of blood *was* concerning.

"As soon as I have her, you help Everest get him to the car," I told Aspen.

He nodded, remaining in wolf form, his ears trained to the door that Kai hid behind.

I approached Asha's designated bedroom, aware that she'd probably heard a lot of the commotion, the fighting and the door crashing. Still, I opened the door quietly.

When the hall light spilled into the room, I saw that Asha was sitting up in bed. The sight of her there nearly made me fall to the floor.

She gasped when she saw me and leaped from the bed. I met her halfway, dropping so that her small arms could reach my neck and then I stood, spinning her around, tears streaming from my eyes while she squealed with excitement. I didn't think she'd ever held onto me so tight.

"Daddy! You're here!"

"Surprise baby," I managed to say. "I finally came to get you."

"Now?" she demanded, pulling back. "Hang on."

She wriggled free of my arms and ran to the light switch, turning it on. We didn't have time to linger but I was helpless to stop her as she ran around the little room, collecting pictures she'd drawn and the stuffed animals that had gone missing with her.

"Okay! Ready!"

Chuckling, I bent down, scooped her into my arms.

"There's a bit of a mess out there," I warned. "I want you to close your eyes, okay honey?"

She gave me a dubious look, but perhaps since she hadn't seen me in a while, she decided not to argue, burying her face in my neck as I caried her out.

"Is he okay?" I asked uneasily.

Seymour's eyes were closed now, but I could see his labored breathing.

"I don't fucking think so," Everest said. He looked like he was going to be sick.

"Don't worry," Aspen said, shifting back to human. "I could hear his heart beating strong. Come on."

He waved me past, helping Everest to lift Seymour.

Understandably, they didn't wait for me as I tucked Asha into her seat. She was sleepy but wide eyed, staring around at us curiously.

"Why did you come get me at nighttime?" she asked, yawning. Clearly, she had no clue what the heck was going on. Honestly, I was glad for that.

"I'll follow you home and watch the house," Aurora said from behind me. "Just in case they have someone come after you."

I swallowed and nodded.

"If you don't mind."

She nodded, going to her car to tail us.

Worry for Seymour was eating at me, but I just had to trust that they got to the hospital on time because once we got home, Asha was so excited to be there, running around, pulling all her toys out of the toybox, begging for TV.

I didn't usually let her stay up late, but I didn't even think of dampening her happy spirit.

When she finally started to settle down, snuggling up against my side on the couch and asking for her favorite show, I put my arm around her small shoulders and kissed the top of her head.

Finally, I texted Everest for an update and immediately received a response that set me at ease. *The doctors are working on him now.*

I let out a relieved sigh and let my head fall on the back of the couch, absently watching Asha's show with her.

I was exhausted. The stress of losing her, and now losing Ember right when I got her back... I wasn't quite sure how to handle it. I needed to be here for her now, but as soon as she was safe, I'd be out there again, finding Ember.

It struck me then: Alvy. The man had found my kidnapped daughter in less than twenty-four hours. Surely finding my runaway mate would be even easier.

I sent him a message and settled back, glad I had at least done *something*.

Whenever Asha fell asleep, I would have to ask Aurora to come inside and keep watch over her while I left to hunt my lover down.

"You smell different," Asha mumbled. She turned her sleepy face, pressing it against my chest, unable to reach my scent gland with her small stature.

I wiggled down on the couch, allowing her better access. Her little nose rubbed against my gland, comforting her with my familiar scent. I wrapped my arms around her, knowing that my close presence like this often made her fall asleep.

"You smell sweeter," she decided.

I knew she was smelling Ember on me. His scent was fully laced into mine. I loved it. How long would it take, I wondered, for Ember's scent to fade into nothing but a memory?

"I met someone," I said softly, "while you were gone."

She was silent for a moment.

"Is that why you couldn't come get me?"

I shook my head, tilting her chin so that she met my gaze with wide eyes that were suddenly glassy.

"No, love," I said. "Ember would never have kept me from you. He wanted to be a family with me *and* you."

"Really?" she asked, hesitantly. "But where is he?"

"He left so that I could get you back."

She fell silent for a moment, a frown pulling her brows together before the thoughtful expression morphed into a smile.

"Well, I'm here now, so he can come back!"

Despite myself, I smiled.

"You're right," I said.

I stroked her hair back.

"Can you tell him to come back now?" she insisted.

"I'll go get him in the morning," I promised.

She smiled.

I was beyond grateful that somehow, she really had been treated alright. She seemed to be her usual self. There was no sign of trauma in her behavior. I was going to get every last detail about her time with her kidnappers before long, with the help of a therapist if necessary, but for now I could rest easy.

Luckily, it didn't take long after that for her eyes to droop and her body to go slack with sleep.

I carried her up to her bedroom and carefully tucked her in. God, I'd missed the simple things so much. There was nothing like almost losing someone to make you appreciate every little detail. The way her face relaxed with sleep, wrapping the thick blanket around her small form, the soft sounds of her breathing...

My heart could barely take how happy I was to have her back.

Once I found Ember and had him here, safe and warm and loved, I couldn't imagine that I would ever want anything else in life.

Chapter Twenty-One

Ember

The cold was an unpleasant familiarity.

It was the later part of spring, the chill of winter lingering, but a long time ago I had noticed that even in the heat of summer, being on the streets made you cold inside. It was psychological, I guessed, but either way, here I was again, and I was freezing.

I'd taken the new clothes that I had been wearing plus one of Coal's coats from the closet. I hoped he wouldn't mind. I hadn't been able to resist and I was glad for that now, because the oversized jacket felt almost like a blanket. Coal's scent was strong on it too. It was so comforting. I pulled the hood up and breathed him in, even though it made my heart ache.

It was going to rain later. The afternoon sun had risen, casting a gray light over the streets that wasn't much better than the dark of night. At least in the darkness I could blend into the shadows.

Today, my first day back out here in so long, I felt like I was on display.

I tried to ignore the feeling, taking a seat on a bench across from the Belfort Hotel, where I had spent years living off and on. More off than on. The place was just as ratty as ever.

I didn't want to have to check in tonight.

In my dream world, I would find Asha today, before nightfall. I would run home to tell Coal and by this evening, we would all be together. Everything would be perfect.

But if I didn't find her today, I would stay in the Belfort for a couple of nights, I decided. Just a long enough to stay warm and gather money.

A laugh burst from my lips.

Wasn't that what I'd always told myself?

I had always had dreams of finding somewhere better, not just better to stay but better for my whole life.

But... one small thing *had* changed that I could

possibly take advantage of. I had been mated. I was in fresh, clean clothes. Maybe I didn't look like a street rat anymore. Maybe someone would give me a job.

My heart raced a little at the thought. It would be nice to have some sort of purpose or goal now that I was not going to be a family omega.

My heart squeezed.

I hadn't allowed myself to even imagine having pups with Coal. I'd never thought of raising any children, but we would have had Asha right away. We would have had a real family.

That's why you're doing this, I told myself, *so that Coal can have that, at least. Even if its without you.*

"Hey, what are you doing sitting here? You get sick of the psycho already?"

My stomach dropped as I looked up. I hadn't noticed the man standing in front of me. My gaze met his narrow eyes and the guy smiled. My skin crawled at the familiar face.

"What do you want, Lambert?" I asked, keeping my voice steady. "I thought Coal already taught you a lesson."

He glanced around at the mention of Coal's name, but seemed satisfied that he wasn't nearby.

Still, he pulled the collar of his jacket up to hide his face.

"He's insane," he said, voice low. "You would have done so much better with me. I mean, who the fuck leaves their new mate alone on these streets? Did you decide to chuck him already?"

He laughed at the idea.

I opened my mouth, ready to defend Coal, but an idea struck me.

Lambert was in on the whole scheme, wasn't he? Maybe he knew something about Asha's whereabouts.

He was cowering slightly and kept looking around like he expected Coal to jump out from behind a garbage can or bush.

"How did you get roped up in all of that, anyway?" I asked, trying to keep cool even though my heart was racing.

Lambert grit his teeth.

"My family... they didn't approve when I joined the fight league. Thought it was too low class."

I arched a brow, surprised that he of all people could come from high stock.

"The guys saw that I had potential. They wanted to hone my skills. Get me on top. Of course. It helped that I sweetened the pot with a payout."

I held in my disgust. The fact that he had to buy his way into good fights meant that he probably didn't have much potential at all, but I kept that opinion to myself.

"Still have plenty of it," he said, leering. "Money, I mean. You want me to give you some company?"

I frowned, surprised that he was trying for this right in the middle of the day and in the open. He must have been desperate, I realized.

Was that why he was here? To find an omega to get through an oncoming heat with?

Shit. Did I still look like I belonged out here, selling myself for chump change? Or was he asking because he knew where I had started? All bait wolves were taken off the streets, it was a badly kept secret, after all.

"Come on," he said, voice low. "You look cold. I'll warm you up at least. I just need a couple hours. I'll get us a room. You can keep it for the night."

His scent spiked, hitting my nostrils. He didn't smell bad or anything. All alphas had a slightly intoxicating note to their scents, especially when they were in rut—and he was fast approaching that. It was already starting and unless I went along with him, he was probably going to spend it alone, which could often be unbearable.

I didn't give a fuck of course, but if I didn't do something soon, he might leave without telling me anything useful.

"What about Asha?" I asked, cutting to the chase.

"I'll tell you anything you want to know," he said, eyes slightly wild. "I'll tell you where she is. *After*."

My heart jumped into my throat.

Coal would hate this.

I hated this.

But.

This was my last chance at the life I had been teased with. And hadn't I slept with more alphas than I could count? What was one more?

I bit my lip and stood.

"Just a couple hours," I said. "And I want money."

Lambert lit up and reached out, grabbing me by the wrist harder than necessary, as though he thought I was going to take off.

I allowed myself to be dragged across the street and into my old haunt. My eyes darted around, heavy with the feeling that my shame was being watched. I didn't see anyone though, just the usual figures sitting on vents and the odd business person hurrying by. The bell jingled as the heavy glass door swung shut on its hinges and the familiar moldy smell of the carpet hit me and nearly made tears spring to my eyes.

This was not what I had seen happening upon escape from the cells. I'd happily thought this part of my life was behind me.

For coal, I found myself saying silently. *For Asha.*

The receptionist, a bone-slim beta who was missing half of her blackened teeth, caught sight of me and grinned.

"I thought you'd be in the bottom of a ditch by now!" she laughed. "Where you been?"

Lambert, my alpha of the hour dropped money on the counter and snatched the key she offered, pulling me to the stairs before I could think of an answer.

"Come on," he muttered gruffly. The smell of his rut, his arousal, was growing with each step, the anticipation clearly turning him on, but it was making me feel sick.

I stumbled on the top step, nearly falling, but he didn't care, dragging me along, showing his nasty nature once more.

"Hurry up."

When we got to our door, his scent was overwhelming, and tears started to blur my vision.

Fuck. I can't do this.

Lambert didn't notice my hesitation though, pulling me into the room with a groan and tugging me against his body, to rut his hard cock against me.

His scent was *everywhere*, and the lovely, comforting smell of Coal would be washed away by this man that I didn't even know.

"Stop."

He didn't seem to hear me.

"You smell like *him*," he growled. His fist gripped my hair, yanking my head back as he sniffed my neck.

His eyes blazed orange. Alphas didn't like when their lovers—temporary or not—smelled like other alphas.

"Have you two been fucking recently?"

Shaking, I lifted my hand, pulling my collar down to expose Coal's bite mark, still fresh and slightly tender to the touch.

"Of course," I said proudly. "Coal is my *mate*. Not you. Now get your hands off me. I changed my mind. I can't do this."

Somehow, I managed to shake him off, stumbling just out of his reach.

He bared his teeth, fangs extending. An obvious threat.

"It's too late now," Lambert said. "I don't have time to find anyone else. You made your choice."

"It's your own fault you left it so long," I snapped.

"Because your alpha got in my fucking way when I was going to take you the first time," he snarled. "It's time for retribution!"

Suddenly, he lunged for me. But I was no spring chicken. I'd been in situations like this more times than I could count, and my reflexes were trained for it.

I ducked down, missing the alpha's extended claws and diving out of the way.

I ended up standing in front of the bed, facing him as he swung around to face me. He leaped, catching me just as I tried to jump out of the way again. The door was clear now, I just had to get to it —but Lambert caught me by the sleeve and threw me onto the bed.

I hit it, landing on my back as panic surged through me and Lambert landed on top of me, pinning me down with a hand on each shoulder. His lips pulled back in a snarl, claws digging into my bones, not quite breaking the skin—yet.

"Stay still and shut up," he growled.

He bent down, as though the matter was dealt

with and bit my neck—too close to my scent gland. Anger surged through me. I couldn't let the bastard taint Coal's mark on me. I didn't want anyone else!

Fuck! Why had I been so stubborn?! I should have stayed with Coal. We could have faced all our struggles together, as a family. After all, that was what we were. A day running around pretending to be homeless wasn't going to change that.

I didn't need the big house. Coal was my home.

If I had been thinking straight, I would have known—I was Coal's home too. My stupid self-doubt be damned. We *were* all each other needed.

My hand reached out blindly, found something cool and hard, and without thinking, I gripped it and slammed the thing as hard as I could against the alpha's head.

The lamp—it turned out—smashed against his skull and immediately he fell limp, his heavy body crushing me.

Chapter Twenty-Two

Coal

I was already scouring the streets when Alvy's call came.

"I've got him."

My heart nearly gave out from the relief.

"He's okay?"

There was a brief silence, then Alvy's even voice saying, "He seems to be."

"What does that mean?" I demanded.

"He's being approached by someone—an alpha."

"What? What the hell does he want?"

"I can't hear them," Alvy said. "They're discussing something. It looks serious."

"Shit," I muttered.

Alvy was silent on the other end, obviously watching the exchange closely.

My body itching for action, I started running even though I didn't know where they were.

"Fuck, where are they?"

Alvy let out a low breath.

"Sorry, Mr. Kent, the guy is taking him into the Belfort."

Fury hit me like a hurricane.

I nearly stumbled from the weight of it.

Ember *wouldn't* go willingly. I knew he wouldn't. Some alpha asshole was about to force himself on my mate. Couldn't the bastard tell that Ember was already taken?

I was already running. I was two blocks away. At first, I'd felt bad that, when Ember went missing, I immediately turned to the roughest streets in town to look for him, but it looked like I knew my mate better than I thought. He'd gone to what was familiar. Perhaps simply for the comfort of it, but now that we were mated, could Ember really find comfort anywhere that wasn't by my side? I knew he couldn't.

The hotel was there, just in sight. Across the street, I saw Alvy's nondescript figure, an average type of man that could easily blend into a crowd.

He didn't move forward to help me, but there was no need.

This pushy alpha was going to shit himself when he saw me coming for him—for good reason.

I burst through the front door, making the receptionist jump with a startled yelp.

"I'm looking for my mate. His name is Ember."

The roughened woman paled.

"I don't want any blood on the carpets," she said.

She knew Ember—of course. He used to live in this hellhole—and she knew he was here. I didn't have time for games.

A growl tore from my throat and she stumbled back, putting more space between us.

"Room seven."

I took off down the hall, up the narrow, moldy staircase just as my nose caught Ember's scent.

I shifted, the need to go faster pushing me and I reached the door for room seven just as—it swung open.

Ember hurried out, stumbling at the sight of me, shocked.

For a moment we stared at each other. I was just

as off guard as my mate was. Then Ember burst into tears and hurled himself at me, throwing his arms around me and burying his face into my thick fur.

I shifted and twisted until I could pull Ember into my arms, holding him tightly as he choked and sniffled.

"You big brute, what are you doing here?"

His frustrated words didn't have any effect when he pressed kisses to my neck, where his face was buried.

I pulled him in even tighter. Anxiety twisted in my gut because Ember smelled like someone else. An alpha in rut. The scent was all over him although, I realized, not strong enough for them to have slept together.

I pulled back, forcing Ember to meet my gaze with glassy eyes. I was afraid to ask but forced the words out.

"I'm here to bring you home. My contact saw you going in here with an alpha."

Ember's cheeks darkened.

"Old habits die hard," he said. "I thought I could get info from him the same way I always used to get a bed to sleep in... but I couldn't go through with it."

My whole body sank with relief.

"He let you leave?"

Ember laughed.

"Hell no. I knocked him out."

For a moment, I stared at Ember, shocked as his words rang in my head.

"Wait. Information?"

He bit his lip, looking up at me like he thought I was about to get mad.

"It was Lambert. He said he knew Asha's location."

Unable to believe it, I let go of him and walked to the room he had just left. The door was still wide open and sure enough, there was the bastard I'd thought I'd already dealt with lying face down on the bed, the smashed remnants of a table lamp littering the cushions around him.

I considered carrying out my promise and killing the persistent asshole, but he looked so pathetic lying there that it didn't seem worth the hassle.

Impressed, I looked back at Ember, who shrugged.

"He was a bit heavy, but I wiggled out from under him," he said nonchalantly. "I may be your omega, Coal, but I can take care of myself too."

I nodded.

"Evidently."

Ember wasn't like the omegas I'd known in my

life. He wasn't the sweet, quiet type that had been sheltered forever. He was a strong, independent man who deserved to be respected for all he'd been through and especially for his strength.

"I've been an idiot," I said. "I was trying to shelter you. I didn't want you to worry so I hid what I was planning from you."

Ember frowned, watching me, waiting.

"I had a P.I. following the men who took Asha. He found her and, last night, I got her back."

Ember's hands shook when he reached forward, putting them on my arms.

"Are you for real?"

I nodded.

"She's home, Ember. She's safe. All that's missing is *you*."

"What about the fight league?" he asked, voice trembling. "They want a lot."

"I arranged a trade with Abram," I explained. "I'm going to fight for you, Ember. Literally."

Ember stared, a fresh wave of tears filling his eyes.

I pulled him into a tight embrace, squeezing my eyes shut.

"I'm sorry," I whispered and then, unable to

stand the other alpha's scent any longer, I pressed my face into his scent gland, scenting him.

Ember shivered.

"Please tell me you'll come home," I begged.

Ember nodded.

"I thought that being there... I thought I was in the way."

"I'm sorry," I whispered again. "You're not in the way. You and me and Asha are family."

Apparently, that was the right thing to say, because Ember took a shuddering breath and nodded.

"Let's go home."

Chapter Twenty-Three

Ember

Coal's hand in mine was a warmth that I would never let go of again.

It was a shift deep within that started with all the jagged parts of me finding their matches and becoming smooth. It came with a confidence that everything would be okay. That together we were strong enough to take on the world, our pasts, and our futures. None of it would hold us back from the happiness we found together.

The whole ride home, our eyes kept finding each

other, locking for moments that seemed to last forever.

"I love you," I found myself saying. Like it was nothing. Like it was as simple as stating the weather, and it was.

The car jerked though, someone honked, and with red cheeks, Coal pulled onto the side of the road and put on the hazard lights before looking at me.

His eyes shone but no tears fell. I didn't need that, but the warm embrace that Coal pulled me into, now *that*, I did need.

I clung to him, tense until Coal returned the sentiment.

"I love you too," he said.

He kissed my cheek, but that wasn't enough so I turned, angling for more and sighing in relief when our lips met.

It was just like all the others, warm and full of passion, and I realized then what had been weighing on my mind.

"You really don't mind, do you?" I mused.

Coal parted only far enough to meet my gaze.

"Mind what?"

"What I did back there—what I used to do... I

didn't think you'd want to kiss me or touch me right away."

"You said you didn't—"

"I didn't," I confirmed. "Not even a kiss. I tried to get away before he even dragged me into that room."

I shook my head, unfortunately remembering the other alphas I'd had the displeasure of knowing over my lifetime.

"Still, you're not as possessive as I expected of an alpha that I'm mated to. I've heard stories of omegas not even allowed to be *seen* by other alphas."

"Don't get me wrong," Coal said after a moment. "I don't want that ever happening again but—the only reason you were out there was because I messed up. I didn't share everything with you the way that I should have. I want to change that. I want us to be completely open with each other."

Surprised and a little moved, I shook my head.

"You still say that, even though now you know the full truth?" I swallowed and forced the conversation we'd skirted around since meeting. Call me a masochist, but I was sure Coal would eat his words and prove me right about alphas.

"I fucked more alphas than I could possibly even remember," I said. "When I was in heat, they wouldn't pay me because they were *doing me a favor*. The rest of the time, I did it for food or for a place to stay... I've been the bottom of the barrel, Coal. At least you did something with your life. I just became a whore."

Coal was deathly still, his scent thick with anger and hurt. It made my head spin, but I waited. Neither of us pulled away.

"I wasn't as bad off as you. I was an adult by the time my dad vanished and left me to fend for myself. I even had a job doing security overnight while Asha slept... You, on the other hand..."

He shook his head, the anger intensifying. I wanted to pull back, but I couldn't bring myself to move.

"The system let you down," Coal finally said. "The dregs of Lunar City found you and made you a victim. It almost killed you."

I blinked, the reality that Coal was not angry with *me*, but at the fact that I had been put in that position, made my eyes sting all over again. Coal was right. None of it had been fair.

"I thought that night—" I choked, unable to go on for a moment. "I thought the fight night would be my last. Instead, I found you."

"We found each other," Coal corrected. "We get another chance to live the life we want. Together."

"I don't know how I got so lucky."

"I'm the lucky one," Coal said. "Somehow I went from nearly losing everything to gaining everything."

My heart warmed.

When we finally collected ourselves enough to get back on the road, it only took a few more minutes to get back to Coal's house—our home.

As soon as we walked through the doors, the sound of kids' shows on the TV and the smell of something delicious reached us.

"Oh, looks like your daddy's home," a female voice said from the direction of the living room and a little girl squealed.

Excitement and nerves bubbled up inside me as the cutest little girl I had ever seen came bounding to me. She came to about my waist, with long, tangled brown waves and huge gray eyes, the same color as Coal's.

I found myself lowering to her level, meeting her curious gaze as she stopped in front of me.

"Are you Coal's mate?" she asked, appearing very concerned.

I nodded.

"Yes," I said somberly. "I'm Ember. I've heard a lot about you."

She watched me for a long time, searching my eyes. Finally, a tentative smile lit her face.

"So, you're going to stay with us?"

I found myself glancing up to meet Coal's warm gaze before I nodded.

"If you don't mind having me," I said. "I'd love to be part of your family."

She seemed to consider for a moment and then nodded, reaching out and suddenly gripping me by the hand and pulling me along after her.

"Come on," she said, waving Coal along and then turning to explain to me, "we're watching my favorite movie!"

Coal's friends were sprawled out on the couch, filling the living room with their large forms.

They all looked tired but smiled when they saw me.

"Looks like the lovebirds are back together again," Everest said, standing. "Glad you're back home."

I smiled, touched that they cared.

I'd never had friends who would show up like this, right when they were needed.

"How is Seymour?" Coal asked gravely.

Everest's normally bright gaze dropped to the carpet.

For a moment, he couldn't speak.

"Still hasn't woken up," Aspen said, coming up behind him and patting his shoulder. "But he will, right buddy? That's what the doctors said."

Everest swallowed, looking unconvinced, but nodded.

"I'm going to go check on Glen," he said. "He's choked about all of this."

"I can't imagine," Aurora said sadly. "Danica would be inconsolable if I got hurt like that..."

She stood, patting Everest on the back.

"I'll go home to her, and then we'll meet you at Seymour and Glen's place with some dinner."

"We'll probably be at the hospital," Everest said.

She nodded.

"I'll come visit too," Coal said, but Everest shook his head.

"Come tomorrow. Spend the day with your family. You deserve that."

Coal pursed his lips but nodded.

They said their goodbyes to Asha and left us.

The three members of our new family, together for the first time ever.

Coal pulled us over to the couch, settling Asha in between us.

"What happened to Seymour?" I asked when Asha got absorbed in her movie again.

"He got shot helping me get Asha back," Coal said quietly. "He's in a coma."

My jaw dropped, and he met my gaze, all the guilt and fear clear in his expressive eyes.

"God," I whispered, "I'm so sorry."

"I should have gone alone."

I shook my head.

"I get feeling that way but, I'm sure he wanted to be there. He knew the risks, right?"

Coal shrugged.

"He has a mate at home, waiting for him."

I squeezed his arm.

"I'm sure he'll wake up. I have a good feeling about it."

That seemed to mollify him. He snuggled closer to us, turning his attention back to the TV.

Asha was into her movie, but every time something big happened she either repeated it or tried to explain it. Seeing as I had never seen this rainbow unicorn show before, she seemed intent on helping me understand.

Once she finished telling me about the horns kind of being like magic wands, Coal leaned close, breath tickling my ears.

"What do you think?" he asked.

There was an anxious note to his voice. He didn't need to explain how much my answer meant to him.

"I already love her," I said honestly.

Coal took a deep, slow breath and relaxed. All the pent-up worry and stress from a hard few days melted out of him just like that. Just because I was here to say the right thing.

Likewise, I could feel myself healing, love and hope for the future filling all the wounds that I'd been left with.

Maybe we would have issues. After all, no one got through life completely unscathed, but I knew deep in my core that it didn't matter. We would enjoy the good and bad together.

We were getting the chance to live the life we *wanted*, not the one that had been dealt to us, and what I wanted was to be right here.

Chapter Twenty-Four

Coal

"We shouldn't be doing this," Ember gasped.

I ignored him because he was wrapping his legs around my hips and climbing me like I was a fucking tree. The Redwood nickname had all new meaning now. I laughed, lifting him up and walking him to the wall to better the angle.

My pants were already down, discarded somewhere on the other side of the room, and Ember's clothes were all off.

Perhaps the most delightful part of him gaining weight was that he didn't mind me seeing him anymore and the sight of his naked body, all that smooth skin, draped in my arms, thighs flexed around my waist to keep him up, pink nipples hard was enough to nearly undo me.

I pressed my tip to his entrance, not pushing in even though he was desperate for it.

"You sure we shouldn't be doing this? Because we can stop now," I teased.

He grinned.

"You bastard," he moaned, pushing down onto me.

My head fell back as he took me in, engulfing my entire length in his tight, wet heat.

"Fuck," I groaned, "Ember. You're so perfect."

He bit his lip, gripping my shoulders to ride me, his face twisted in concentration and pleasure.

I held on tight, letting him take what he needed.

When his hole tightened around me, his bouncing motions slowing, I watched mesmerized at the look of rapture as it crossed his face. The way his eyes closed and lips parted, the soft, satisfied sounds he made... Watching Ember come was one of my favorite pastimes.

I pressed my face to his neck, inhaling him and then could resist no longer, moving my hips into him until I was coming too, releasing deep within him, just how he liked me to.

His arms came around my neck, holding me tightly so that he wouldn't fall.

"Don't knot me," he panted. "We don't have time."

No sooner had he said it than the door to the change room swung open.

"Shit!" Everest shouted, spinning around to shield his eyes. "Guys, what the fuck! There's like five minutes until the fight starts!"

I pulled out, setting Ember carefully down on his feet.

He scampered around the room, pulling his clothes hastily back on, ignoring the liquid sliding down his thighs.

I licked my lips, watching it. Still panting, I pulled my fight outfit back on.

"All good," I said when we were dressed. "You can look."

Everest was bright red, but he gave us both a scathing look.

"You know you're not even supposed to have sex leading up to a fight," he said, "let alone immediately before it."

I shrugged. "Can you blame me?"

Ember touched my arm.

"I'll go get my seat," he said, lifting to kiss me quickly. "Good luck!"

I watched him taking off down the hall, smiling and shaking my head.

I could hear the crowd, feel the energy from the stadium buzzing through the entire building.

I put my arm around Ever, sighing.

"You'll understand once you have a mate," I informed him.

He rolled his eyes but didn't argue.

He hadn't been quite the same since Seymour had ended up in the hospital. He was still there now, a month later with no signs of waking up soon.

Guilt ate away at me. I didn't and *couldn't* make it better, not for Everest and not for Seymour's mate Glen either. But I also hadn't lost hope the way the Everest seemed to have.

"Where's Glen?" I asked.

"At his seat," Everest said. "I got him one next to Ember so that he wouldn't be alone."

It didn't seem like the poor omega was ever alone now that Everest had taken it as his responsibility to be there for him. I bit my lip, once again unsure how or *if* there was a way to make him feel better. There was nothing I could say though, so I patted his back.

"Ready for your big moment?" Everest asked. "At least you'll have Abram off your back after this."

I nodded.

"He wouldn't be able to drag Ember away from me anyway."

Everest smiled dryly just as I heard my entrance song start.

"Let's go," I said.

I started down the walkway, meeting the rest of my team at the entrance into the stadium.

Together, we emerged into the crowd of thousands as they erupted into cheers.

In the distance I could hear the commentators announcing my arrival and my specs.

This was the part where, normally, I soaked in the atmosphere and felt that adrenaline buzz.

Except, it felt different now.

It felt like... like I'd already won.

I smiled, high-fiving the fans whose hands were close enough to reach as I got to the cage.

On the other side, my opponent was waiting. An up-and-comer who had clamored and run his mouth leading up to this.

All his words and insults had bounced off of me like nothing, because—

I caught sight of Ember, sitting in the first row.

It was like my eyes snagged on his form wherever he was. Even in a room filled with thousands of people, Ember may as well have been the only one there.

He was everything.

Aside from him and Asha, nothing else mattered. Not these fights, not winning, not money.

He grinned and pointed to the cage as though to say, *Pay attention!* and I laughed out loud.

There was no bait wolf used this time. I'd insisted on it and was glad to see that my request had been met.

Instead, our gates opened and we both entered.

I could see the fire in my opponent's eyes, the ferocity and desire to win and that was when it hit me that I didn't feel that way anymore.

Fighting couldn't be my outlet anymore because, well, I didn't *need* one.

He lunged at me, tackling me to the ground in human form and landed atop me, hitting me repeatedly across the face.

And yeah, that hurt, so I made myself move and act. My body, primed to what I had done for years, acted quickly.

I struggled to flip him, but once he was on his

back under me, I returned his strikes as hard as I could.

He thrashed under me. For a moment, I thought the ref would end this, but then, suddenly, he flipped onto his back and bucked me off.

I landed with a thud that winded me but rolled out of the way before he could land on me.

Suddenly, we were on each other, clawing and biting, fur flying.

Neither of us stopped.

Suddenly, I *couldn't*, because I could still see Ember out of my peripheral, watching with his hands over his eyes. He didn't want to see me get hurt and I couldn't let him.

So I kept fighting, relentlessly using my size and determination to crowd my opponent until he was in a corner, still fighting back weakly as the crowd roared around us, chanting my name—*Redwood, Redwood, Redwood*—until finally, he fell limp.

The moment he did, the ref moved to pull me off, but I was already stepping back, shifting to my human form and pumping a fist in the air.

I turned in a circle, arms out, soaking in the raving applause.

I appreciated it. The support I'd received from the people of Lunar City was unmatched. And I would never forget how good it felt in this moment, having won for the last time in front of them all. In front of *Ember*.

When I opened my eyes, he was watching me, grinning happily. Our eyes met and I couldn't look away until the commentator shoved a microphone in my face and a camera blocked my view.

"Congratulations, Coal! How are you feeling?" he asked enthusiastically.

"Great!" I said into the offered mic. "But I couldn't have done it, and I wouldn't even be here, without the help of my team and my friends. Especially Everest, Aurora, Aspen, and my buddy Seymour, who is currently in the hospital."

"And your mate?" the commentator asked, giving me a cheeky smile.

I shrugged as the crowd laughed and jeered. Of course, they'd all seen our meeting, I couldn't play it cool now. Nor did I want to.

"I would definitely be in a dark place right now without Ember," I said, pushing the camera aside so that I could see him again.

He had a camera pointed at his face too and was bright red, but his gaze never left mine.

"Thank you for being here," I told him.

He swallowed and nodded, mouthing, *I love you.*

I chuckled and shook my head.

"Love you too," I said and the crowd *aw*'d.

"Who would you like to fight next?" the announcer asked.

I took a breath, faced the camera, and said, "No one. I think it's time to retire while I'm still on top."

I wouldn't be for much longer if I kept going anyway. My heart just wasn't in it anymore. It was seated with my mate in the front row.

As shock reverberated through the room, I thought carefully of how to phrase the next part.

"I've had a great fight career, but there are other things that need my attention now. But I will always thank the people of Lunar City for supporting me the way you all have. You're the best fans in the world!"

The crowd erupted, giving me one last boost of support while the commentator went on about my legacy, about how I'd never lost a fight. I didn't care. I was already getting out of the cage and marching up to Ember.

He stood up, coming to meet me halfway and pretty much jumping into my arms.

"What was that?" he demanded into my chest. "I didn't know you were quitting."

"Neither did I," I admitted. "But enough is enough. There's something else I have to do now."

He looked up at me curiously, but I didn't want to say too much here.

"Let's just say that Abram isn't going to be very happy with me soon. I have a lot of connections in high places now."

Ember arched a brow, but when I didn't answer, he shook his head, smiling up at me.

"You've been nothing but surprises since you fought your way into my life," he informed me. "All good ones, don't worry."

"Good," I said, grinning and bending to kiss him.

He held me tight, not letting me pull away too soon.

Neither of us even minded the cameras.

"Come on," I said, finally pulling back. "I promised Asha a mac-n-cheese bake."

His eyes glinted.

"Yum, let's go."

Hand in mine, we left the stadium to head home, just like that.

It was all so simple and so easy being together. That was how the good things were supposed to be. And it didn't get boring. Staring into Ember's eyes alone could easily entertain me. But there was more to it.

Together, we were finally the people we were meant to be, living the lives that we deserved.

Despite the situation it came from, I would forever be grateful for the turn of events that put Ember into my cage that night.

Epilogue

Ember

I zoomed Asha around the yard on my back while she giggled like a maniac.

The summer sun was beating down on us and I was sweating and going at half the speed of when I'd started playing with her twenty minutes ago, but she didn't seem to care.

"Again!" she shouted.

How was it that someone so small had so much more *energy*?!

"Okay, enough torturing Ember," Coal called from the deck. "The barbecue's ready."

We both cheered as I gratefully set her back on her feet.

Her plate was already made. Coal always fed her first because her attention span meant that she would sit at the table for all of one minute waiting, and by the time we arrived with the food, she was upstairs coloring on the walls.

She took the plate and then set it down to run to her play slide with the corn on the cob in hand.

Coal shook his head, watching her sharply.

"Don't go down while you're eating!" he warned.

"I know!" she said.

"You should know that she knows everything by now," I chastised, hiding a smile.

Coal smacked my ass playfully.

"Don't start."

I was going to reply but his hand lingered, giving me a little squeeze. I jumped, biting back a yelp as his fingers went a little too precisely into my crack.

"Hey, not in front of Asha," I reminded him.

He chuckled.

"Sorry. I'm still getting used to the bubble."

I bit my lip, trying not to smile too much.

Admittedly, the extra weight had done good things to my body. For the first time, I was feeling confident because I looked so healthy.

And happy too. I couldn't pretend I didn't look like I was walking on air every time I looked in a mirror now.

My eyes looked more alive; the way I walked was lighter. Even my hair was bouncy and shiny.

And yes, I'd somehow gotten a bubble. The universe just kept bestowing gifts upon me. Most notably, the man at my side and the family that I would now do anything for.

We sat down at the picnic table, under the wide umbrella to eat.

As usual, I was too distracted by Coal's cooking to do much talking.

"This steak is divine," I informed him around a mouthful. "Asha! You're missing out, come have the rest of your food."

"Okay!" She slid down the slide, yes, with a mouth full of food while Coal grumbled and watched to make sure she didn't choke, and came to sit next to us.

As we sat there, the three of us together on such a nice, simple day where no one would have to do anything they didn't want to do or go hungry or cold, it hit me how different life now was.

I felt sorry for the old me. The one who thought that isolation in the woods was the only way I would have freedom. I hadn't even known how good life could be, how peaceful.

"What are you thinking?" Coal asked.

I glanced over to find him watching me and smiled softly. He'd probably noticed that I'd stopped eating. That wasn't like me.

"I was just thinking... how lucky I am," I said, my gaze falling to Asha.

She had taken me in as completely as Coal had.

"I have so much now," I said.

"It's what all omegas deserve," Coal said firmly, and my affection for him grew another size.

He'd become laser-focused on his new goal: to remove the bait wolves from the fight league.

After that, I wondered if he would single-handedly try to clean the streets too.

He would do anything to make up for the past I'd had, even though none of that was on his hands.

His compassion was moving.

I reached out, squeezing his thigh under the table.

"You're right," I said, simply supporting him.

I would do whatever I could to help, but my heart was here, in this yard with these two wonderful people.

I placed a kiss on top of Asha's head and then leaned toward Coal for one from his lips.

He gave me a gentle peck and it still made my stomach flutter even though it wasn't new anymore. Everything Coal did made me feel warm and loved.

"What are you two *talking* about?" Asha demanded, and we both chuckled.

"Stuff you'll never have to worry about," I promised.

Afterword

Thank you for reading Bait Wolf! I hope that you liked our first foray into Lunar City because there's more on the way!

Here's a peek at book 2:

Blurb:

Glen

My mate is in a coma.

The doctors say it's time to pull the plug, but I can't bring myself to do it, even though seeing him like this is torture, and going through heats with his prone body is even worse.

I'm not ready to let the life that was taken from us go.

If not for my mate Seymour's best friend Everest, I don't know what I would do.

Everest

It's grief that brings us together.

I would never want to take Glen away from Seymour, but the fact is, he's already gone.

I've lost my best friend, my confidant, my *everything*. And Glen feels the same way.

I can't stand seeing the person that made Seymour so happy suffering like this and yeah, maybe there's comfort in the fact that we both loved Seymour. Glen is the only person who feels this loss the way that I do. That's why it makes sense for us to lean on each other... to *love* each other.

But a mating bond is forever, and the one thing neither of us truly planned for was what we would do if Seymour *woke up*.

Shifting Alphas is an mmm omegaverse romance set in the world of Lunar City. It features two strong alphas who used to be each other's everything and the omega who can bring them all back together. Can they have it all while navigating the dark world of the fight league and each other's hearts?

Don't worry, this book is NOT a love triangle.

Link:

https://books2read.com/shiftingalphas

I will also have a short based in the world of Lunar City featured in Fated and Claimed 2.

Link:

books2read.com/fatedandclaimed2

About the Author

Sienna Sway is a Canadian with her head up in the clouds. Books and writing M/M are her lifelong passions. She has always adored scifi and fantasy and is currently living her dream by writing these books. Thank you for your support!

Join her newsletter for monthly m/m recs and updates, or follow her at any of the links below!

Newsletter: http://eepurl.com/g-E5oH
Website: www.siennasway.com
Patreon: https://patreon.com/SiennaSwayBooks
Facebook fan group: www.facebook.com/groups/
outofthisworldmm/
Instagram and twitter: @siennasway
TikTok: @siennaswayauthor

Also by Sienna Sway